"Should I Have Put A Sign In My Window Back Home— Husband Wanted?"

"You didn't have to leave to find a man." Jace was glaring at Celie.

"Right. Like Logan Reese or Spence Adkins. Lots of temptation there. A convicted felon and a surly cop. Who else is there?"

"Guess." His chest was heaving and his eyes glittered fiercely.

Suddenly, Celie felt an intensity, a hunger, a need that rocked her. She felt the power of masculine desire, pure and simple. And very definitely directed at her.

By Jace Tucker?

She stared at him, her heart hammering, her mouth opening and closing like a fish. "G-guess?" she gasped, looking around wildly. Her mind buzzed. Her blood roared.

Then, desperately, she lurched past him, wrenched open the door and shot down the hall. Someone called after her, but there was no way on earth Celie was stopping now. Not even for the cowboy of her dreams....

Dear Reader,

Summer vacation is simply a state of mind...so create your dream getaway by reading six new love stories from Silhouette Desire!

Begin your romantic holiday with *A Cowboy's Pursuit* by Anne McAllister. This MAN OF THE MONTH title is the author's 50th book and part of her CODE OF THE WEST miniseries. Then learn how a Connelly bachelor mixes business with pleasure in *And the Winner Gets...Married!* by Metsy Hingle, the sixth installment of our exciting DYNASTIES: THE CONNELLYS continuity series.

An unlikely couple swaps insults and passion in Maureen Child's *The Marine & the Debutante*—the latest of her popular BACHELOR BATTALION books. And a night of passion ignites old flames in *The Bachelor Takes a Wife* by Jackie Merritt, the final offering in TEXAS CATTLEMAN'S CLUB: THE LAST BACHELOR continuity series.

In *Single Father Seeks...* by Amy J. Fetzer, a businessman and his baby captivate a CIA agent working under cover as their nanny. And in Linda Conrad's *The Cowboy's Baby Surprise,* an amnesiac FBI agent finds an undreamed-of happily-ever-after when he's reunited with his former partner and lover.

Read these passionate, powerful and provocative new Silhouette Desire romances and enjoy a sensuous summer vacation!

Joan Marlow Golan

Joan Marlow Golan
Senior Editor, Silhouette Desire

Please address questions and book requests to:
Silhouette Reader Service
U.S.: 3010 Walden Ave., P.O. Box 1325, Buffalo, NY 14269
Canadian: P.O. Box 609, Fort Erie, Ont. L2A 5X3

A COWBOY'S PURSUIT

ANNE McALLISTER

Published by Silhouette Books

America's Publisher of Contemporary Romance

For Lyle May,
cowboy and friend

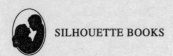 **SILHOUETTE BOOKS**

ISBN 0-373-76441-3

A COWBOY'S PURSUIT

Visit Silhouette at www.eHarlequin.com

Printed in U.S.A.

ANNE McALLISTER

RITA® Award-winning author Anne McAllister has never managed to pigeonhole the sorts of stories she likes to write. Right now she's working on her next Special Edition and Presents novels, both coming out at Christmas 2002, so she doesn't have a lot of spare time. But if you write her at P.O. Box 3904, Bozeman, MT 59772 (SASE appreciated) or e-mail her at anne@annemcallister.com, she promises to answer. Even if you don't write, drop by and visit her at www.annemcallister.com. You're always welcome!

Dear Reader,

If anyone had ever told me I'd write fifty books, I wouldn't have believed them. There was a time I didn't think I'd get through the first one!

It seemed so daunting—trusting two characters I barely knew to find their way to true love and take me along for the ride. What if they got lost? I wondered. What if they expected *me* to help them find their way? What if they decided they couldn't stand each other? Or, worse, what if they fell madly in love on page 19? What was I going to do for another one hundred and seventy or so pages?

But the desire to find out what happened between those two people was greater than the fears about the answers to those questions. And so I began....

A year later (it takes longer when you only write during your two-year-old's naptime), I had a book. Amazed and pleased, I sent it off to a publisher and did the smartest thing I've done in my career—I started another book. I stopped thinking about the first one and got busy on the second. I found new characters to fascinate me, a new story to develop, and I started to write.

I've been doing that now for a lot of years. The two-year-old grew up. Lots of characters have told me their stories and I've enjoyed a lot of happily-ever-afters. But the most exciting one is always the one I'm working on now.

I hope you enjoy Jace's pursuit of Celie in my latest CODE OF THE WEST story, *A Cowboy's Pursuit*. He's been in love with her almost as long as I've been writing books, and he's finally going to get a chance to win her! Meanwhile, I'll be at work on the next one.

I couldn't possibly write a hundred, could I?

All the best,

Anne McAllister

One

The slam of the back door stirred Artie Gilliam from his catnap in the armchair in his living room. He blinked, glanced at his watch, then frowned as he heard booted feet cross the kitchen and stomp in his direction.

"Bit early for lunch, ain't it?" he said when Jace Tucker appeared, glowering from the doorway. "Or did my watch stop?" His daddy had given it to him right after the First World War and Artie supposed it could have given up the ghost by now, but he hoped it hadn't. He was counting on something outlasting his ninety-year-old bones.

"I didn't come for lunch," Jace growled. He stalked into the room, still scowling, his hands jammed into the pockets of his jeans, his shoulders hunched. He strode clear to the end of the room before he turned and nailed Artie with a glare. "She's back."

"She," Artie echoed with interest. It wasn't a question. He knew damned well which "she" Jace meant.

As far as Jace Tucker was concerned, there was only one female in the whole universe: Celie O'Meara. Not that Jace had ever said as much to him. Or to anyone.

If there was ever anyone more likely to make a hash of his love life—besides himself, Artie reckoned, and that had been a good sixty-odd years ago now—it was Jace. For a smart, good-lookin' feller who oughta be able to sweep a woman off her feet without half tryin', Jace didn't have the skills of a push broom.

Artie sighed inwardly and shook his head.

Misinterpreting the head shake, Jace enlightened him. "Celie," he spat.

"Ayah." Artie tried to look as if he hadn't already figured that out. He smiled gently. "How nice."

Jace's shoulders seemed to tighten more. "Ha," he said. He did another furious lap around the living room. The young fool would wear out the rug at the rate he was going, and that would be something else that wouldn't survive him, Artie thought glumly.

Now he raised his brows. "Thought you was lookin' forward to her comin' back."

Jace, being Jace, of course, hadn't said anything of the sort.

But every day when he'd come back from working at the hardware store or from training horses out at the ranch, he'd asked if Artie had heard from any of Celie's family. The whole O'Meara clan had gone to Hawaii ten days ago for the wedding of Celie's sister, Polly, to Sloan Gallagher.

Artie was sorry he'd missed it, but the ol' ticker had durn near give out on him this past winter, and the doc had said he wasn't up for flying halfway around the world yet. Didn't matter, really, as they'd kept him posted. He'd heard all about the wedding on the beach and the party with Sloan's film crew afterwards, and he'd always shared the news with Jace.

He'd relayed every scrap of information he'd got after phone calls from Celie's mother, Joyce; from Polly and Sloan; from Polly's oldest daughter, Sara; and once from Celie herself.

"Huh," Jace had said when Artie told him about Celie's phone call. "Managed to tear herself away from all those beach bums long enough to see if you were still among the livin', did she?"

Artie had grinned. "She's a sweetheart, all right," he had agreed, knowing that wasn't what Jace had meant at all.

Jace had scowled then.

Jace was scowling now, hands jammed in the pockets of his jeans as he rocked back on the heels of his well-worn cowboy boots.

"Reckoned you'd be glad to see her," Artie said, lifting a quizzical brow.

"That was when I thought she'd come to her senses!" Jace's boots came down flat with a thump.

"What do you mean?" Artie frowned. "She didn't cause no problems at Polly and Sloan's weddin', did she?"

Everyone in Elmer knew that Celie had had a crush on cowboy-turned-actor Sloan Gallagher for years. She'd even bid her life's savings to win a Hollywood weekend with him at that cowboy auction they'd held back in February.

What's more, she'd won! But if she'd gone out there starry-eyed over Sloan—and Artie wasn't absolutely sure she had—she'd sure seemed to come back cured. She'd had nothing but good things to say about Sloan, but she'd treated him more like a brother after that.

And a good thing, too, as Sloan had been sweet on her sister, Polly. It could have been sticky, but it hadn't been. Far as he knew Celie had been delighted to be asked to be the maid of honor at Polly and Sloan's wedding.

"She behaved herself at the weddin', didn't she?" he demanded now.

"Guess so." Jace turned and glowered out the window. He rubbed the back of his neck, clenched his fists at his sides, then hunched his shoulders again. To an old rough-stock rider like Artie, he looked exactly like a bull about to blow.

"She ain't gone back to hankerin' after Matt Williams!" he said, aghast.

Matt Williams had jilted Celie ten years ago. At the time she'd been little more than a child—barely twenty and be-sotted with a foolish footloose boy who didn't know a good thing when he had it. But telling her so hadn't helped. Matt's rejection had liked to killed her. It had sure as shoot-in' made her scared of trustin' men.

To Artie's way of thinking, if you got bucked off, you had to just get right back on again, meet other guys, go out on dates. But Celie hadn't seen it that way. She'd holed up with her magazines and her videos and had spent the past ten years dreamin' about Sloan Gallagher.

As far as Artie knew, she hadn't had a date since Matt had dumped her—not until February, anyway, when she'd got up the gumption to bid on Sloan. Of course by then Sloan had already set his sights on Polly.

Artie hoped to goodness that, her dreams of Sloan thwarted, she hadn't decided to start thinking about Matt again.

"Make more sense if she had," Jace muttered.

That made Artie's brows lift. "Since when did you be-come a Matt Williams fan?"

They'd been buddies back then, of course, Jace and Matt—traveling partners, in fact—going down the road from rodeo to rodeo. But Jace hadn't agreed with Matt's way of breaking his engagement. Of course, that could have been because he'd left it up to Jace to call Celie and tell her it was off.

"Matt's a jerk," Jace said now. He yanked off his straw cowboy hat and raked a hand through his hair. "But then we all know that."

Artie had a terrible thought. "She didn't get engaged to no surfer!"

Jace snorted. He scowled. He strangled the brim of his hat. "No."

"Well then, what the devil's the problem? She's back. It's what you been waitin' for." He held up a hand to forestall Jace's protest. "Don't tell me you two are fightin' already?"

It wasn't any secret that Celie and Jace didn't see eye-to-eye. Course that was on account of Celie always having been a sweet, proper-brought-up girl and Jace being something of a hell-raiser. And if that hadn't been enough, Artie knew Celie had always considered Jace the inspiration for Matt's going astray.

"Matt's role model," she'd called him. *Role model* was one of the nicer terms she'd used.

And there was some truth to her accusation. Any young cowpoke with a hankering for women and the wild side could've learned a few things from Jace Tucker. Even now he still liked to have a good time. But he'd settled down a good bit, to Artie's way of thinking.

The Jace he'd got to know over these past few months drank a few beers and shot a few games of pool at the Dew Drop, but he never came home drunk—and he *always* came home. Didn't bring no girls with him, either.

He was true to Celie. Not that she knew it.

Jace wasn't the sort of feller who wore his heart on his sleeve. Most of the time, Artie reckoned, the young fool had it wrapped up in barbed wire and duct tape and buried it under six feet of sarcasm. So it wasn't real surprising that Celie didn't think he had one.

"You two," Artie muttered, shaking his head in dismay as Jace began pacing again, "are enough to try the patience of a saint. You ain't seen her but a few minutes this morning, Jace! You couldn't have, bein's how it's only just past ten o'clock. So what the dickens has she done to tick you off now?"

"She's leavin'!"

"What?"

"You heard me. She's leavin'!" Jace looked halfway between angry and anguished. His blue eyes, generally light and sunny as a summer sky, were now the color of a storm. He flung his battered hat onto the davenport and cracked his knuckles furiously.

"What the devil do you mean, she's leavin'? Where in tarnation would she go?"

"Remember her singles cruise?" Jace fairly spat the words.

Artie's eyes bugged. Of course he remembered the singles cruise. When Celie had come home from her weekend in Hollywood with Sloan, heart whole and over her crush at last, she'd been determined to get on with her life.

Jace, who had darned near driven Artie crazy all the time she was gone, had barely breathed a sigh of relief when he'd discovered that just because Celie was over Sloan, it didn't mean she was going to fall into *his* arms.

No sir. Instead in April she'd gone on a singles cruise.

"What the hell does she need a singles cruise for?" Jace had wanted to know. He'd been doin' laps in the living room then, too.

"What indeed," Artie had murmured, "when she's got a single feller who loves her right here?"

Jace had stopped dead at that. He'd spun around and

leveled a glare at Artie. ''What the hell are you talkin'
about?''

Artie, no fool but no chicken, either, had shrugged
lightly. ''Seems to me it's obvious,'' he'd said.

A muscle had ticked furiously in Jace's jaw. He'd ground
his teeth, but he hadn't denied it. He'd rubbed a hand
against the back of his neck and had shaken his head as if
to clear it. And then he'd dug the toe of his boot into the
rug and muttered, ''Damn fool thing to do.''

''Is this the singles cruise we're talkin' about or you
bein' in love with Celie?'' Artie had asked with a smile.

''What do you think?'' Jace had muttered.

He was muttering again now.

''Don't see how she can go on another one,'' Artie said.
''Them things are expensive.''

''She can afford it,'' Jace said through his teeth, ''if they
hire her.''

''Hire her?''

''That's what she came in this morning to say. Just
waltzed in, pretty as you please, and handed in her notice.
'Just wanted you to know I'll be leavin' in two weeks,''
Jace mimicked Celie's soft tones. '''Got a job on a cruise
ship,''' Jace went on in the same furious sing-song voice,
'''so I won't be around to annoy you anymore.''' He
slammed his fist into his palm to punctuate the end of the
quote.

Artie's heart kicked over in his chest. It worried him a
little when his heart did that, but not as much as he was
worried about Jace. And about what Jace would do now.

Artie might be closing in on ninety-one, but he wasn't
dead yet. He remembered what it felt like to look at a
woman and want her. He remembered what that hungry,
hollow feeling was like, how it made a guy follow a woman
with his eyes and fall over his own feet if he wasn't careful.
He'd done it a time or two himself.

That was one of the reasons, after his heart attack, that he'd taken Jace on to work for him. To give him a chance.

Even though she had her own business—C&S Spa and Video, where she cut hair and gave therapeutic massages and Sara, her niece, rented videos—she still came in most mornings and worked at the hardware store with him.

Artie knew she could have handled the store when he'd had his heart attack. That was the kind of girl Celie was—thoughtful, generous, kind—the sort who'd do an old man a favor, who'd help out wherever she could. The sort of gal who would make somebody a good wife.

Who would make Jace Tucker a good wife.

When Artie saw that Jace was sweet on her, Artie reckoned the least he could do was to throw them together. So he had.

He'd got Jace to fill in for him when he was in the hospital. He'd acted weaker and more frail than he really was when he came home, all so's those two could spend some time together and get their love life sorted out.

But they hadn't.

Two more stubborn people than Celie O'Meara and Jace Tucker—when it came to falling in love—would be hard to find. Celie persisted in believing that Jace was no different than he had been at twenty-three, and Jace persisted in remaining stubbornly silent instead of admitting how he felt. They'd been working together four months now, almost five. And as far as Artie could see, things had gone from bad to worse.

Well, maybe Celie's new job would be the wake-up call, Artie thought, taking a deep breath and sitting up straight. Maybe Jace would finally say something that would stop her from going.

"So," Artie challenged him, "what're you gonna do about it?"

Jace slapped his hat back on his head and jerked it down

hard. "Get drunk," he said furiously. "Then go find me some other girl!"

He turned on his heel and banged out the door. All the windows rattled.

Artie sighed and shook his head. Life really was wasted on the young.

For as long as she could remember, Celie O'Meara had been in love with the idea of love and marriage. As a little girl, she'd played "wife" and "mommy" while Polly and Mary Beth had played cowboys and Indians and doctor and nurse. It was possible, she thought when she was being brutally honest with herself, that she'd still been "playing" the role when, at nineteen, she'd got engaged to Matt.

She hadn't thought so at the time, of course. She'd thought she loved Matt Williams. Worse, she'd thought he loved her.

She had been devastated when he'd jilted her. Her world had come crashing down. All her hopes, her dreams, her expectations had been destroyed. She'd felt like a fool.

Even more, she'd felt like a failure. In Celie's mind, Matt's rejection had publicly branded her as a woman unable to satisfy a man.

"You've just got to meet some other guys," her sister Mary Beth had said, doing her best to console her.

"Better guys," her sister Polly had insisted firmly.

"Exac'ly. It's like fallin' off a horse," Artie Gilliam had told her. "You jest gotta pick yerself up an' get back on."

"Of course you do. And you will. You'll find the right man someday," her mother had said, then she'd given Celie a hug of encouragement.

But Celie wouldn't even look. She wasn't about to "get back on." She'd been humiliated once. She'd trusted a man. She'd given him her heart and he'd trampled it into the dirt. Get back on and let another one do the same thing?

No way. Once was enough for any lifetime, thank you very much.

But even though she'd vowed never to trust another man, her old dreams of love and marriage had died hard. In fact they hadn't died at all. And even though Celie had given up on "real men," she'd kept her fantasies.

Like Sloan Gallagher.

Sloan was everything she'd ever dreamed of in a man. He was handsome. Strong. Brave. Resolute. Clever. Determined. Sexy.

But mostly he had been safe.

She'd seen him in theaters and on television, had read about him in magazines and allowed herself to imagine what loving him would be like. It had been wonderful—because it had been impossible—until Sloan agreed to come to Elmer for the Great Montana Cowboy Auction to save Maddie Fletcher's ranch.

Then Celie's fantasy world had collided with her real one. Her two-dimensional Sloan was in danger of becoming a real person. Her dreams were no longer merely dreams, they were possibilities—if she let them be. For weeks before the auction they had tormented her, taunted her, challenged her. And in wrestling with them, she'd realized what a hollow empty place her real life had become. She might have been able to ignore that realization, to pretend it didn't matter—if it hadn't been for Jace Tucker.

She might have been able to ignore herself—but she couldn't ignore Jace.

No one *ever* ignored Jace!

He was too vital, too intense, too…too everything. She remembered him from childhood, watching him from afar, always aware of him—*wary* of him—because he seemed different. Fascinating. Bigger, tougher, louder, rougher. Alien. Other.

Unlike Polly, who had been her dad's sidekick, and Mary

Beth, who had tagged along after them, Celie had always been a "girly" girl. She'd never been entirely comfortable at the brandings, hanging around the fire teasing with the cowboys. She'd never wrestled with the boys on the playground. She'd liked Matt because he hadn't been as rough as some of them. He'd been quieter. Gentler.

A man after her own heart, she'd thought.

But even Matt had rejected her.

And it had been all Jace Tucker's fault! Matt had come home from the Wilsall Rodeo that summer, saying he'd been talking to Jace and he was thinking maybe he'd go down the road with Jace for a spell.

"Sow me a few wild oats," he'd said with a grin, "before you tie me down."

She should have worried then, but she hadn't. She hadn't believed he really meant it. But she also hadn't been thrilled about him going down the road with Jace Tucker.

"Don't let Jace lead you astray," she'd warned him.

And Matt had laughed. "No fear."

But it turned out that all her fears had been realized when two months later Matt hadn't come home to get married. Instead, fifteen minutes before the ceremony was to start, Jace Tucker had called to say Matt wasn't coming.

"He says he's not ready," Jace had told her.

"What do you mean, not ready?" Celie could still remember her high, tight voice. But even then she'd been like an ostrich, head in the sand, believing that Jace must mean that Matt simply hadn't figured out how to tie his tie or button his suit coat yet.

"To get hitched," Jace had spelled it out. "He says he can't do it. That he's got places to go, things to do, to see..." Jace's voice had faded, and there had been a considerable pause during which he obviously expected her to say something.

But Celie had been incapable of speech.

She'd been strangling the receiver in disbelief. There were close to a hundred people just up the street going into the church at that very moment, for goodness' sake!

Her mother had been calling to her to get off the phone and hurry up. Her dad had been standing in the doorway wearing a wholly uncharacteristic suit and tie of his own as he'd grinned at her.

But Celie hadn't grinned back. She'd stood there staring at the phone in disbelief, listening to Jace Tucker sigh and mutter under his breath, then say, "For crying out loud, Celie, say something!"

"It's a lie," Celie had said, because that was all she could think right then. This was Jace, after all! She knew Jace would think getting married was a joke. She hated him right then more than she'd ever hated anyone.

"It's not a lie, Celie," he'd said, his voice harsh. "Matt isn't coming! He doesn't want to get married. Call the wedding off."

Mortified, she'd banged down the receiver. Then, numbly, she'd done exactly that. And all the while she'd burned with a white-hot fury at Jace's impatience. As if she should have known! As if she should have been expecting it. As if it were obvious that no man in his right mind would want to marry her!

Jace hadn't even said he was sorry.

Why should he be? He'd been with Matt the last time they'd come through Elmer. He'd stood in the kitchen, shifted from one booted foot to the other, impatient to be gone, barely even looking at her. He'd obviously thought she was a loser from the very start. And somehow he'd managed to convince Matt.

He'd influenced Matt. *Inspired* Matt!

And Celie still resented that. But mostly she resented Jace because every time she saw him she was reminded of her failure.

She was not the person she wanted to be. She was a reasonably successful businesswoman. She was the owner of Elmer's only hair salon and video store. She was a volunteer at the library, the doting aunt of six nieces and a nephew, and the person that Sid the cat liked better than anyone else on earth.

But she didn't have a boyfriend. Or a husband. Or a child.

She wasn't a wife. Or a mother.

She was a reject. And every time she saw Jace Tucker, she remembered that.

For most of the past ten years she hadn't had to see him. Footloose rodeo cowboys like Jace didn't hang around hair salons in Elmer, even if their sister and her family still lived on the family ranch five miles north of town. A year could go by and she might only catch a glimpse of him once or twice.

She heard about him now and then, of course. She knew he'd done well over the years in rodeo. He'd never been the world-champion bronc rider like Noah Tanner, who lived west of Elmer. But he'd got to the National Finals several years, and this past year Celie knew he'd gone to Las Vegas in the number-one spot.

"Jace says this is his year," his sister, Jodie, who was Celie's age, had said proudly when she'd come into The Spa just before Thanksgiving to get her hair cut. "Maybe if he wins in Vegas next month at the NFR he'll retire and move back to town."

Celie's heart had jerked in her chest at the very thought of running into Jace Tucker every time she turned around. But she hadn't said a word. She'd kept right on clipping, pleased that at least her fingers hadn't jerked.

"Maybe he'll be ready to settle down," Jodie had speculated. "Find himself a good woman and have a passel of kids."

Celie couldn't help snorting at that.

Jodie had looked in the mirror and their eyes had met. She'd smiled mischievously. ''Maybe I'll send him around.''

''No, thanks,'' Celie had said as fast as she could get the words out of her mouth.

''You used to think he was sort of cute,'' Jodie reminded her. That was the trouble with living in the same place your whole life. People remembered all kinds of foolishness— like the fact that in sixth grade at a slumber party Celie had once let slip that she'd thought Jodie's big brother was kind of cute.

''I've developed a bit of taste since then,'' Celie had said sharply.

Jodie's brows lifted at Celie's tone. ''He's not that bad,'' she'd defended her brother.

You could also count on Jodie *not* remembering that Jace had been the one who'd broken the news to Celie about Matt. Unless he hadn't told her.

Of course he'd told her! Celie couldn't imagine that he wouldn't have. But she didn't say anything. She made herself focus on Jodie's hair again, only replying, ''I'm not interested in your brother.''

She had, however, said a fleeting prayer that Jace Tucker would *not* become the World Champion Bronc Rider in December. And she remembered feeling a momentary pang of guilt when a couple of weeks later she heard that he'd been injured at the NFR. She hadn't wanted him to win, but she hadn't expected he'd wind up in the hospital.

Not that it had been *her* fault!

If her God were the sort who exacted divine retribution for such selfish behavior, though, putting Jace to work in the hardware store after Artie had his heart attack would have been right up His alley. But if Celie wasn't blaming herself for Jace's getting injured, she could hardly blame

God for Jace being in the store on that January day when Artie had had his attack or for his being with her at the hospital when the old man had been determined to have someone take over the store.

It hadn't been necessary!

Heaven knew she could have handled the hardware store herself. She'd said so. But Artie hadn't listened. He was stubborn and set in his ways, and even though he counted on Celie and her mother and her sister and nieces to do a lot of things, he was obviously old-fashioned enough to think a man ought to be in charge.

He'd thought *Jace* ought to be in charge!

Since then she'd had to deal with Jace Tucker. And it was having to deal with Jace on a daily basis that had made her furious enough to bid on Sloan.

Seeing Jace day after day, being treated to his teasing, his knowing winks and gleeful grins had driven her right up the wall. A day hadn't gone by that he hadn't made some remark about Sloan Gallagher—and her!

Celie had seethed and fumed. She'd felt first hollow and then angry and then desperate. She'd tried to cling to her dreams, but reality—and Jace—had kept getting in the way.

As the Valentine cowboy auction had drawn closer, Jace had even turned up in her dreams as often as Sloan! It was transference, she'd assured herself. He was good-looking, damn him, though she'd never ever admit that out loud. He had thick dark hair and blue eyes very much like Sloan's. But while Sloan's were warm and tender—at least in his films—Jace's laughed and crinkled at the corners whenever he grinned and teased her, which was almost all the time.

Celie wanted to throw things at him. She wanted to kick his shins. Mostly she tried to stay out of his way. But that didn't mean she didn't notice him.

How could she not?

And when he wasn't teasing her about Sloan, he was

busy flirting with all the women who came into the store.
There were, it seemed, hundreds of them. Not just the locals
girls, whom he flirted with as a matter of course, but all
the ones who'd come to Elmer to bid on Sloan.

"You'd think they came to bid on you," she'd said to
him once.

"I'm not for sale," he'd said smugly.

"No one would buy you," she'd retorted.

Jace had just laughed. But Celie hadn't thought it was
funny. She also knew it wasn't true. If Jace Tucker had
been auctioned off, she was quite sure lots of women would
bid on him. He'd certainly had plenty of women clamoring
to stay with him in the extra rooms at Artie's house while
they waited for the auction.

Celie had muttered something disparaging about Jace
and his harem in the days right before it.

He'd just laughed. "Jealous? Want to join?"

"Never!" Celie had snapped. "I won't share my man."

"If you ever get another one," Jace said. He'd said,
"Sorry," quick enough right after, when he'd seen the look
on her face.

But the shock of what he'd said had struck her to the
core.

And that was when Celie had actually begun to consider
bidding on Sloan. At first the idea was so wild and preposterous that she couldn't believe she'd ever thought it.
But the more she did think about it, the more she realized
that she had to do something. If she didn't, they'd be nail-
ing her in her coffin and they'd write on her tombstone,
"Here Lies Cecilia O'Meara—She Died Before She
Lived."

And Celie wanted to live.

Fantasies weren't enough anymore. Dreams didn't suf-
fice.

And so, on the day of the auction, she'd mustered her

courage, marched into the town hall and had bid her bank balance on Sloan Gallagher down to the last red cent. She'd won. She'd been panic-stricken.

And yet, it had been worth it—just to see the look of utter disbelief on Jace Tucker's face.

The memory of it could still make her smile. It had been so supremely satisfying, so uplifting, so utterly pleasurable. It was actually addictive, she discovered, the joy of shocking Jace. She'd wanted to do it again.

Of course if Sloan had fallen in love with her, no doubt she would have seen Jace's jaw dragging on the ground. But Sloan hadn't.

And just as well, because while she liked him a lot, she found that she didn't love him.

Certainly not the way her sister Polly loved him. And not the way Sloan loved Polly.

But seeing them, she knew she wanted that kind of love. She didn't want to be alone for the rest of her life, didn't want to be a spinster hairdresser with no one to love but her cats.

So she made up her mind to keep looking.

Going on a singles cruise in April had been a step in that direction. It had been so completely different from her land-locked, down-home existence that it had seemed like the next logical step for a woman who was trying to jump-start her life.

And it had had the added advantage of flabbergasting Jace Tucker once again.

"A *singles* cruise?" He'd stared at her as if she'd announced that she was going to dance naked on the counter in the middle of Gilliam's Hardware Store. As if a singles cruise was out of the question for a woman like her.

As if she wouldn't know what to do there!

Celie had known what to do. And if she had been scared spitless the day she'd boarded that giant ship in Miami, she'd soon discovered that it wasn't as terrifying as she'd imagined. She'd discovered that the skills she'd developed while talking to people when she cut their hair were useful when she wanted to meet new people, when she wanted to meet *men*.

She'd met quite a few men. She was still wary. Still nervous around them. But she was never as nervous with any other man as she was around Jace Tucker. She'd hoped the cruise would cure that.

But it hadn't. She'd hoped he'd go back to the ranch and she wouldn't see him and it wouldn't matter. But he hadn't done that, either.

"Artie wants me to stay," he'd said. "And Ray and Jodie's is a little too small for us all. I'll stay with Artie while I'm building my place."

His place. He was settling down, just the way Jodie had said. He'd told Celie so himself. He'd even implied he had a particular woman in mind. But he wouldn't tell her who.

And Celie couldn't guess. It seemed to her that every time she saw him he was with someone else—from her niece Sara to the actress Tamara Lynd, who'd been one of the women staying with him during the auction.

Was it Tamara? She refused to ask. But she didn't want to be around to watch, either. And that was when she'd decided that a job on a cruise ship might not be a bad idea. So she'd set about making it happen.

She was thirty. She wanted a life. She wanted a husband. A family. And taking a job on a cruise ship had seemed as good a way as any to make that happen. So she'd applied and crossed her fingers and hoped.

And last night when she'd got back from Sloan and Polly's wedding, there it was—the job offer she'd been waiting for. The very thought of going terrified her.

But more than that it gave her enormous pleasure—especially this morning when she'd told Jace Tucker she was leaving Elmer for good.

Jace should have known better.

By the ripe old age of thirty-three he should have figured out that drinking himself under the table was a less than successful response to almost anything that ailed him—and that included getting Celie O'Meara out of his mind.

She was out of his life. Had been for a month. A month that seemed like a year. Ten years. Forever, when you got right down to it.

He still couldn't believe she'd left! If ever there was a homebody in the world, Celie was it. But twenty-four hours after she'd come home from Polly and Sloan's wedding she'd put a Going Out of Business sign in The Spa window and seven days later she was gone.

"She didn't even say goodbye!" Jace had said, outraged, when he discovered it.

"Because you were still in bed," Artie told him with blunt disapproval, "sleepin' off that bender."

It was true that Jace had been doing his fair share of drinking at the Dew Drop and down at The Barrel in Livingston since Celie's announcement. He'd also been doing his best to find a woman who appealed to him more. He hadn't, but it wasn't for lack of effort.

"You mighta stopped her," Artie had told him reprovingly.

Jace had scowled. "Yeah, right. Begged her not to go."

Artie nodded. "Yep."

But Jace would never have done that. He wouldn't have admitted anything—not when she'd acted like he was lower than dirt. "I'd have looked like a damn fool."

"And now you don't?"

No, damn it, he didn't! He just looked tired.

He still looked tired a month later—because, damn it, he

was tired. It was a lot of work going out every night, carousing, meeting women, trying to be flirtatious and charming, *especially* when he didn't want to bother, especially when it didn't seem to be doing any good!

Artie was disgusted with him, and Jace knew it. The old man didn't say anything, but he didn't have to. He only had to sit there in his damned recliner every evening with that book of zen wisdom Celie's mother had given him in his lap, regarding Jace with sad resignation over the tops of his spectacles as the younger man headed for the door. It was Nickel Nite at the Dew Drop, which meant that women could play pool for a nickel a game. With luck there might be a new one—one single, reasonably attractive, interested female that he hadn't already met.

"What?" Jace demanded, glowering at Artie's pained expression.

But Artie only shook his head. "I'd think you'd get tired of it."

He didn't have to specify what. And Jace was tired of it. But he didn't see any alternatives.

"You got any better ideas?"

"Could be."

Jace stopped, his hand on the doorknob. He gave Artie a hard look. "Which means?"

"Life is what you make it."

He had the blinkin' zen book on his lap again. Jace ground his teeth. "Sure it is," he spat.

Artie nodded, smiling. "You are what you do."

"I'm *doin'* something!"

"Getting drunk. Picking up women. *Trying* to pick up women," Artie corrected himself, infuriating Jace even more.

"I'm not getting drunk. I haven't in weeks."

"And thank God for that," Artie said piously.

"It didn't hurt *you*," Jace pointed out.

"Didn't help *you,* though, either, did it?"

"Nothin's helping!"

"Seems not," Artie said thoughtfully. He patted the book on his lap. "Maybe you should try somethin' else."

"I've tried."

"Besides other women."

"Like what?" Jace said belligerently. He nodded his head at the zen book. "I suppose that thing has all the answers."

"You could say that."

"Such as?" Jace challenged.

Artie shrugged. "Wherever you go, there you are." At Jace's confused stare, Artie sighed, then amplified. "And if you don't go, well, then you ain't there, are you?"

"I haven't gone anywhere."

"Ain't that the truth," Artie muttered. "Sometimes, I swear," he said with weary resignation, "you are as dumb as you look. You love Celie O'Meara, don't you?"

"Well, I—"

"You love Celie O'Meara." It wasn't a question. "You been tryin' for a month to forget her, to move on, to get her outa your system, outa your mind, outa your life. You tried work, you tried booze, you tried other women. And it ain't done you a damn bit of good. You haven't been able to do it, have you?"

"Well, I—"

"You haven't." Artie answered his own question. "So you gotta do somethin' else. Somethin' to convince her you love her."

Jace opened his mouth to protest, then shut it again. He didn't see how the hell he could convince her—even if he had a mind to—if she wasn't even here. Besides, telling someone you loved her was risky. It meant saying things he'd never said to anyone—least of all the one woman in the world who had every right to hate his guts.

"Course, if you're chicken…" Artie murmured.

Jace's teeth came together with a snap. "Fine. By all means, let's hear it. What do you suggest?" he said. "What zen proverb is gonna make it all better?"

"Ain't zen," Artie said. "It's just good old-fashioned common sense. If the boat don't come to you, boy, it's time you went to the boat."

Two

Working on a cruise ship was totally different from *cruising* on a cruise ship. Celie learned that in about ten minutes flat.

It was long hours spent doing exactly what she'd done back in Elmer—cutting, combing, shampooing and coloring, and two afternoons a week giving massages to passengers hungry for a little pampering—and sometimes doing it with the deck swaying under her feet. It was sharing a room barely big enough to get dressed in, a room so deep in the bowels of the ship that she wondered if she ought to decompress on her way up to the salon where she worked. At work it was a supervisor who didn't carry a whip, but who might as well have. She was called Simone.

"Actually Simon," Stevie, one of the other hairdressers said. "As in Simon Legree."

Celie could believe it. Simone had sacked her first roommate, Tracy, for coming out of a passenger's stateroom one morning wearing the dress she'd worn to dinner the night before.

"You charm the passengers," Simone said. "You don't sleep wiz zem."

Celie took the lesson to heart. Not that she'd had her heart set on sleeping with any of them, anyway. It was enough to be charming. She'd met a lot of people. A lot of men, actually. She'd visited several Caribbean ports on her days off with a few of them. She'd made more memories in the past eight weeks than she'd made in a lifetime in Elmer.

"Aren't you homesick?" Polly had asked her worriedly the first few times she'd called.

And the answer had been yes.

But it was only to be expected, Celie knew. And she told Polly firmly, "I'm fine. I don't have time to be homesick."

It was only the truth.

Besides, even if she did lie awake some nights and think about Elmer and the life she'd left behind, she also knew that staying in Elmer would never have given her what she wanted.

There was no man in Elmer who would love her the way Sloan loved Polly. She knew every man in Elmer, and as far as she was concerned, all the good ones were taken.

She knew there was no hope when she'd called Artie from Kauai to tell him about Sloan and Polly's wedding, about how beautiful it had been, and how wonderfully in love they were. And she'd said, "I hope I find a man like that someday."

And Artie, heaven help her, had said, "What about Jace?"

Jace? She'd practically swallowed her tongue. "Jace?" she'd sputtered. "Me and Jace Tucker?"

"What's wrong with Jace?" Artie had demanded.

Everything, Celie could have told him. Jace was too

handsome, too sexy, too sure of himself, too flirtatious. He also thought she was the dregs of the universe. She was the girl that even a loser like Matt Williams had dumped! She couldn't believe Artie was even suggesting it. Was the old man getting senile at last?

But she couldn't ask that!

"Let's just say it wouldn't work," she'd said finally. "It would be like Little Red Riding Hood and the big bad wolf."

"Well, now—" Artie had begun, but Celie had cut him off.

"No, Artie. Forget it. Don't ever think about it again."

Getting away from Jace's teasing grin and barbed comments had been one of the biggest perks of leaving Elmer. Getting away from Jace was one of her primary reasons for going.

Not that she had been running away! On the contrary, she'd been running toward plenty of wonderful opportunities. She was seeing the world. She was making memories. She was meeting lots of wonderful people. Meeting men.

It was what she'd come for, she told herself. To see the world, to meet new people. To find true love.

Well, she wasn't admitting *that*. Not to anyone else. If the more worldly members of the crew—and virtually everyone on the ship was more worldly than she was—suspected for a moment that Celie had come looking for her one true love, they'd never let her live it down. They already thought her wide-eyed innocence was somewhere between charming and a colossal joke.

Carlos, the debonair, slightly jaded waiter from Barcelona, teased her about it on a daily basis. "Such big eyes you have," he would say, grinning at her amazement at the beauty of places they visited.

"I make her eyes even bigger," Yiannis, the wine steward from Greece, promised. He offered to show her around the "spots the tourists don't visit" in ports they came to.

But Allison, the hairstylist who became Celie's roommate after Tracy got sacked, wouldn't allow it. "You're not going anywhere with him! Spots the tourists don't see, my sainted aunt Effie! And what does he mean by that but sleazy hotel rooms!" She sniffed. "He'd have you naked in five seconds flat!"

While Celie had no desire to go ashore with Yiannis, she felt compelled to protest that she wasn't so foolish as to be talked into a sleazy hotel room or out of her clothes.

Allison had lifted a brow. "Oh, yes? And who was it let Armand take her up on the fantail at midnight to watch the neon fish?"

She could still blush just thinking about that. So there weren't neon fish. Live and learn.

And anyway, she'd come to no harm. Armand, who ran the gifts and precious gems shop on board the ship, had turned into a perfect gentleman when Celie, trapped in his passionate embrace, had slid one knee between his and explained the options facing his own family jewels.

"You're learning," Allison had admitted later.

Indeed, Celie was learning a lot. And in the past two months she'd met a lot of fascinating people from all over the world. She'd seen amazing sights, had sent home a dozen postcards, had determinedly embraced the life she'd let pass her by for the past ten years.

But she hadn't found true love. Yet.

She would, though. She was determined. After all, she couldn't expect to find her one true love just waiting for her to come along, could she? Of course not. It was bound to take a little effort on her part. So she had enjoyed a few ports of call in the company of the opposite sex. Men Allison approved of. Ones unlikely to drag her off to a sleazy hotel room.

"Gentlemen," Alison had said, giving Armand and Carlos and Yiannis a look that would singe the hair on their heads.

They'd backed away, palms out, muttering, leaving Celie to Allison.

"Carlos is a gentleman," Celie had protested.

"Carlos is a Casanova," Allison said firmly. "Not your type. You need a nice man."

As if she couldn't handle any other kind, Celie thought, a little put out. As if she were a novice, barely out of the cloister. As if she needed training wheels.

"Seen any neon fish lately?" Allison murmured whenever Celie grumbled.

So she'd dated men whom Allison approved of. She'd gone to the straw bazaar in Nassau with a charming Scot called Fergus. She'd water-skied in St. Thomas with an Australian named Jeff and she'd drunk margaritas on the cruise line's private island beach with a Canadian called Jimmy.

They were sweet. They were fun. They were "gentlemen." They were certainly better than staying home in Elmer and letting life go on without her.

But none of them was "the one."

What if she never met "the one"? The thought niggled in her brain sometimes late at night. What if she stayed not just weeks or months, but *years* and never met the man of her dreams? It didn't bear thinking about.

It would happen. Of course it would.

Sometime when she least expected it, she would spot him coming onboard, or she'd catch him watching her during her little spiel during the safety section, or she'd look up from cutting hair, glance in the mirror and their eyes would meet.

Just like that, there he would be—the other half of her heart.

And just like that, they'd fall in love, get engaged and go home to Elmer to get married. And this time the whole valley really would get to celebrate as Celie O'Meara got married at last.

And when she came down the aisle toward the man of her dreams, Celie vowed that she'd stick her tongue out at Jace Tucker!

Artie had had some dumb-ass ideas in ninety years. But Jace doubted the old man had ever had a stupider one than this.

So how stupid did that make him for going along with it?

How big a fool was he that he'd anted up more money than he wanted to think about for "seven fun-filled days *and nights* cruising the Caribbean" on the ship on which Celie O'Meara cut hair?

He had to be out of his mind.

"Of course yer outa yer mind," Artie said cheerfully, bright and early the morning he drove Jace to the airport in Bozeman. "We're all fools when we're in love."

In love. He kept stumbling over the idea every time he thought about it. Love was something that happened to other people. Love was something that made their worlds go around—not his. It was something other guys sweated out—not him.

And now? Now he was an hour from getting on a plane and chasing thousands of miles after Celie O'Meara.

He considered backing out.

Artie wouldn't let him. "No, sir. You do, an' you'll regret it."

Jace thought he might regret it a whole lot more if he went. What if he went and Celie took one look at him and turned up her nose and walked away? What if he went, laid his heart on the line and she told him to go to hell?

Worst of all, what if he went and couldn't open his mouth and say a word?

"You?" Artie darn near drove off the road, staring at him when he mentioned that. "Not talk? Huh? Can't imagine it. You ain't exactly no shrinkin' violet, you know."

"Watch where you're going!" Jace growled. It was true, ordinarily he didn't find dealing with women any hardship at all. He could talk to women, he could flirt with them, he could charm the pants off them—literally.

Other women.

He'd never got to first base with Celie O'Meara.

"You never did anything this harebrained, I'll bet," he muttered as Artie took the turnoff to the airport.

There was a long moment's silence—necessary, Jace figured, when a man had ninety years to think back through— and then Artie sighed. "Shoulda," he said.

Jace's eyebrows lifted. "Oh, yeah?"

"Mebbe." Artie allowed, shrugging bony shoulders. "Or mebbe not." He stared straight ahead again, concentrating on making the turn into the airport.

Jace waited for him to elaborate. He didn't.

"Thanks," Jace muttered finally as Artie pulled into a parking space. "You're real encouraging."

"Gave you the idea, didn't I?" Artie said. He cut the engine, grinned and cuffed Jace lightly on the arm. "Give it a shot, boy. What've you got to lose?"

His hope, Jace thought. As long as he didn't confront Celie, as long as he didn't spell out what he wanted, as long as he didn't tell her he loved her, he could still believe they might have a future together.

"Come on." Artie shoved open the truck door. "Git the lead out. Faint heart ain't never won fair lady."

"Wish t'hell you'd stop with this zen stuff," Jace muttered as he climbed out.

Artie gave him a long-suffering look over the hood of the truck. "Not zen. Romance novels."

Jace stared.

Artie gave another bony shrug. "Joyce gave 'em to me. Feller's gotta do somethin' with his time when it's damn near all he's got left. Besides, I believe in love. I believe in you."

Startled by Artie's uncharacteristic words of approval, Jace blinked. "What do you—"

But Artie wasn't waiting around to repeat them. "C'mon." He jerked his head, then turned and tottered, bowlegged, in the direction of the airport terminal.

Jace stood still. His fingers clenched around the handle of his duffel. The grip felt almost familiar, the way his hand had tightened on the ropes of a thousand bucking horses.

"Ride of your life," one of his old rodeo buddies, Garrett King, used to say.

Back then he'd treated each one that way. He'd seen each ride as a step on his way to winning the world. Back then he'd believed he would. With the confidence of youth, he'd been sure he'd succeed. He had grit, he had try, he had talent, he had stamina. Why shouldn't he win it all?

But grit and try and talent and stamina hadn't been enough. There were things he could control and, Jace had realized this past year, things he couldn't.

When he'd had that wreck in December at the National Finals, he'd been so close...so very close to the top that he'd been almost able to taste it. He'd gone to Vegas, dreaming of the day the gold buckle would be his.

And now it never would be.

As long as he'd had his career, he'd had hope. Now he didn't.

He didn't want to admit what he felt for Celie O'Meara—not to Celie, at any rate. Not the way she felt about him. Not until she changed her mind. If he said, "I love you," and Celie said, "I don't love you and I never ever will," that would end it.

He'd have no hopes left at all.

Still, what was he going to do, back out now? Goaded by Artie, he'd already spent the money. And everybody in Elmer knew—again thanks to Artie—that he was takin' a little cruise. Of course Artie had told them all, too, he'd be going on Celie's ship.

If that had earned him more than a few speculative looks from the Elmer gossips, Jace tried not to think about it. But even now he could feel the tide of red creep up his neck just thinking about those two old biddies, Cloris and Alice, clucking and smiling and murmuring about him having "a thing" for Celie O'Meara. He'd tried to ignore them. But they weren't alone in their speculation. Even sensible women like Felicity Jones and Tess Tanner had eyed him up and down last time he went out to the Jones place to deliver some lumber. He'd thought he was imagining their interest until he'd been about to leave and Tess had sung out, "Be sure to get your hair cut while you're there!"

Felicity had even said he might want a massage, too— if Celie were giving them.

Cripes! Just thinking about it made his jeans tight.

But that was sex, not love. This wasn't about sex. Not entirely, at least. What he felt for Celie was more than simple desire. It had to do with things like forever and commitment and waking up together every morning. Still, it was true that he felt plenty of good old-fashioned lust where she was concerned.

Now he thought about getting a massage from Celie onboard ship. Did he dare?

"You comin' or you gonna stand there till you take root?" Artie was scowling at him over his shoulder.

Jace's fingers gripped his duffel even tighter. *Ride of*

your life, he said to himself just the way Garrett used to say it.

He just hoped it didn't grind him into the dirt.

He flew to Salt Lake City, then to Miami. It was hotter than Hades, flat and smoggy when he arrived. Hardly the paradise he'd been promised. But he grabbed his bag off the luggage carousel, mopped his brow with the bandanna tucked in his back pocket, then caught the shuttle bus to the cruise ship where paradise—and Celie—were waiting.

He tried to imagine what she'd say when she saw him. Then he tried not to.

He tried to soak up a little of the atmosphere, smile at his fellow passengers, feel like he wasn't a fish out of water and about to meet up with the fillet knife.

Almost everyone on the bus was staring at him. At his hat. Most everyone was wearing open-necked shirts and golf slacks. A couple of men had flat caps. There didn't seem to be any other cowboy hats in sight.

Jace took his off and rubbed a self-conscious hand over spiky damp hair. He thought he should feel better now, less self-conscious, more part of the group. The truth was he felt bare and vulnerable without it. He felt naked.

And that was the last thing he needed when he met Celie again. He jammed his hat back onto his head. The hell with it. So what if he looked like a cowboy and they all looked like golf club professionals? He *was* a cowboy, damn it. And he doubted, for all their golf clothes, any of them had ever hit par.

He couldn't afford to buy clothes he'd only wear for a week. Besides his long-sleeved, western-style shirts like the one he was wearing, he had packed a polo shirt and a couple of T-shirts, and the travel agent had told him to take a pair of dark slacks. The only pair he had were the ones he'd worn to his sister, Jodie's, wedding ten years ago, to his father's funeral three years back and to the few rodeo functions where jeans weren't acceptable attire. He figured they'd still look new when it came time to bury him. Not that he wanted to be buried in them! Wherever he spent eternity, Jace wanted to do it in jeans. And boots.

He was wearing boots now. He damned sure wasn't buying any loafers with tassels on them. They'd laugh him out of Elmer if he came home with silly shoes like that!

They'd probably laugh, anyway, if he came home without Celie.

Life without Celie didn't bear thinking about.

He tried not to. He tried to muster up a little interest in the people on the bus. Jace generally liked people. He liked talking to them, learning about them, listening to them. And so he smiled at the lady sitting next to him.

"How you doin'?" he said, smiling at her. "This your first cruise? It's mine."

The lady smiled back, stopped looking askance at his cowboy hat and started telling him that it was her first cruise, too, and she'd been saving for it for years. Then two more women jumped into the conversation, and by the time they got to the ship, they were pretty much one big happy family—him and a bunch of women.

Well, they weren't all women, but most of them were. He discovered pretty quickly that unattached single men of his age—or any age, for that matter—were in short supply on cruise ships. A couple of them even asked him if he was an escort.

"An *escort?*" Jace was aghast, and he knew his face was bright red.

The woman who had been sitting in the seat in front of him turned around as they got off the bus. "Not that kind of escort," she said kindly. "But they sometimes recruit gentlemen to come along on cruises for free—as escorts— so we lonely women will have partners to dance with."

"Oh." Jace ducked his head and scratched the back of his neck. "I didn't know. I thought maybe you reckoned I was..." He didn't finish the sentence.

Several of the women laughed, but it was friendly laughter, and one of them—Jace would have sworn—patted him on the butt!

"I wouldn't mind," one said cheerfully.

"Nor me, sugar," added another.

More laughter, and Jace laughed with them. "Thanks," he said, "I'm flattered. But I came to see a friend."

They were immediately all ears. "A friend? A *girl*friend," they said.

"We hope," one of them muttered.

"Yes," Jace said at once. "Well, not exactly a *girl*friend, but—a girl, a woman," he said quickly at a few widened eyes. "Just she's not exactly my girlfriend. Yet."

They were all avid. "Who is she?"

"What's her name?"

"Is she a passenger?"

"No," he said. "She, um, works here."

He didn't want to tell them too much. He didn't want them to know who she was. The last thing he wanted was to conduct his courtship under the watchful eyes of a ship full of eager women. That would be worse than trying to do it back in Elmer!

"Don't press the poor boy," the lady who'd sat next to him said, patting his arm maternally. "You'll make him nervous."

As he moved through the line to get registered and get assigned to his stateroom, Jace was already nervous. The ship was huge. It was like a gigantic, multistory floating hotel. A very ritzy floating hotel. And there were uniformed good-looking guys all over the place, smiling and nodding at the passengers, saying hello in half a dozen foreign languages. They said hello to him, too, even as they blinked at the sight of his cowboy hat.

Not one of them, he noticed, was wearing a wedding ring. They'd probably all come to work here in order to meet women—exactly the way Celie had come to meet men. They probably knew her.

She was probably already in love with one of them!

He tripped over his own boots and almost went sprawling. He would have if three blonde women he'd met on the bus hadn't caught him and hauled him upright.

"You okay, sugar?" one of them asked.

"Fine. Just fine. I—" he fumbled with the map of the ship that the registration clerk had given him, as he tried to get his bearings "—just gotta figure out where I'm going."

One of the blondes peered over his shoulder and studied the map and the room the registration clerk had circled. "Why, you're just down the hall from us." She beamed and took his hand. "I'm Lisa, sugar. Deb and Mary Lou and I will take care of you. Just come along now."

And Jace, feeling as if he'd been tossed from a bronc and landed on his head, gave himself up to the inevitable and did exactly that.

Lisa and Deb and Mary Lou appointed themselves his guardians. They were cousins, all from Alabama, all schoolteachers, all single and in their midthirties. They went on a cruise every summer to spend time together and maybe, just maybe, meet the men of their dreams.

"It hasn't happened yet, of course," Deb said with a fatalistic shrug.

"But we're optimists," Mary Lou said.

"Or masochists," Lisa said wryly.

"Whichever," Deb finished, "we'll keep an eye on you."

"I—" Jace started to protest, because he wasn't the man of their dreams and he needed to be sure they knew it.

Lisa patted him on the cheek as they stopped outside his stateroom. "Don't you fret, now," she told him. "We aren't goin' to poach on some other girl's property. We know you're taken."

"I—"

But Mary Lou nodded in solemn agreement. "Taken. We understand. We're delighted. It's so romantic."

It was?

"Absolutely," Deb agreed and added fervently, "we're just glad to know there are real men like you around."

Jace hoped Celie felt the same way. It still worried him. He'd put it out of his mind as best he could all the way down here. He was committed, he was going on the cruise. But he didn't have a clue as to what to say to Celie when he ran into her.

Hell, the damn ship was so big he reckoned he could go the whole week and never run into her at all. He wondered, for a split second, if he could get away with going home and telling Artie—and the rest of Elmer—that he'd tried to find her, but he'd just never managed it.

Somehow he didn't think it would wash.

He had to figure it out, though, now that he was here. After the Alabama triplets left him, he let himself into his stateroom. It was bigger than he'd imagined, with more closets than his sister's whole house. He set his hat on the desk and surveyed his digs for the week. It wasn't flashy like some of those Las Vegas hotel rooms he'd stayed in. It was more subdued, had more class. The furniture was light oak, the drapes were a soft sky blue. There was a little refrigerator by the desk, thick carpet under his boots, and right in the center, a close to king-size bed.

More than anything else, Jace admired the bed. Used to sleeping on a bunk bed in his nephew, Robby's, room when he was at the ranch or on the hard narrow bed in Artie's spare room when he was in town, he thought the bed alone might be worth the cost of the cruise.

Well, not *alone,* he amended. His mind's eye was already envisioning Celie in it with him. The notion grabbed him, held him. He sank down onto the bed and let the vision play out in his head.

After all, it made sense. If he'd learned one thing in all his years of bronc riding, it was that visualization was a good thing. You'd never get anywhere close to winning the gold if you worried that you weren't going to make the ride. You needed to imagine yourself sticking to the saddle, needed to see yourself doing everything you needed to do to win.

It was way too easy to see himself doing things in bed with Celie O'Meara.

The trouble was that he couldn't quite see all the intermediate steps that he would have to take to get there.

He lay back and folded his hands under his head and tried. He tried to imagine her smiling when she saw him. He'd seen her smile often enough, though rarely at him. He envisioned that smile. He envisioned her saying his name like she was glad to see him. He saw himself reaching for her, drawing her close, wrapping his arms around her. His brain fast-forwarded to them in bed, to him skimming off her clothes, to him shedding his own, to the two of them learning each other's bodies—

A quick staccato tapping on his door made his eyes fly open and his whole body jerk.

He leaped to his feet, heart pounding, mind reeling, body aching. Cripes, if it was Celie— He shut his eyes and prayed for inspiration. Then he ran a hand over his hair, shoved his shirt in his jeans and, wincing, adjusted their very snug fit. It didn't help much. So he grabbed his hat and held it in front of him as he answered the door.

Of course it wasn't Celie. She didn't even know he was here.

The Alabama schoolteachers, all looking cool and fresh in clean, bright dresses, stood beaming at him. "We're headin' off to the safety demonstration. It starts in five minutes. Y'all wanta come along?"

He had to, of course. The safety demonstration or "life boat drill" as one of the crew had called it, was the only mandatory event on the cruise. "I, er…" His voice sounded thick and ragged. He cleared his throat desperately. "Yeah, sure." He took a deep shuddering breath and tried to get a grip.

Mary Lou looked at him closely. "You all right, sugar?'

Feeling like an eighth grader whose brain—and body—were out of control, Jace nodded. "Yeah. I just… Lemme just…wash up a sec. I just sorta…dozed off."

He didn't wait to see if they looked as if they believed him. He ducked back inside his room, shut the door and hurried to the bathroom to splash some water on his face. He toweled it dry, then yanked on a clean shirt, buttoned it and jammed it into the waistband of his Wranglers.

They were still annoyingly snug—because he was still annoyingly horny. He hadn't been with a woman since February. Not since the night of the auction, when Celie had won Sloan Gallagher. Not since Tamara Lynd had walked into his bedroom, slid her arms around him and assured him that Celie wasn't the only fish in the sea.

In a fury because Celie had not only bid on but actually won a weekend with Sloan Gallagher, Jace had slaked his need with Tamara that night.

It had been a disaster. At least for him. He hoped Tamara didn't hate him. He'd hated himself enough for both of them. And he hadn't been with a woman since.

No kidding his frustrated body grumbled now.

He grabbed his Stetson again, but he still didn't put it

on. Instead, with determined nonchalance, he clutched it in front of his belt buckle and opened the door again.

Lisa, Deb and Mary Lou were still waiting with identical smiles on their faces and bright-orange life jackets in their arms.

"Hang on." Jace went back and got his, clapped the Stetson on his head and carried the life jacket in his arms. "All set."

Deb looped her arm through his right arm, Mary Lou clutched his left hand, and Lisa led the way. "Y'all follow me. I've been here before."

The lounge was already full of people. A staff member, smiling brightly, ticked off their names when they arrived and directed them into the room. A handsome, uniformed guy greeted them with a cruise-ship trademark smile, told them his name was Gary and proceeded to run through the safety measures. The point was, if any emergency occurred, everyone was supposed to come here and wait for further instructions.

"Now," Gary said, "we'll just make sure you all know how to put on your life jackets, and then you can get on to the fun part of your holiday."

He demonstrated, putting the jacket on over his head, tightening and fastening the straps. "Your turn," he told them. "If anyone has any problem we've got plenty of staff here who can help you."

It was like the first day of football practice in high school when the coach had handed out the shoulder pads. There was lots of bumping and bumbling as too many people in too small an area raised their arms and fumbled as they put on the unaccustomed vests.

Jace fumbled, too, and, now that his arousal had subsided, wished he hadn't brought his hat.

"Hey there, cowboy, let me hold that for you," a familiar female voice behind him offered.

He turned and found himself staring into the bright, beautiful eyes of Celie O'Meara—a Celie O'Meara whose cruise-ship smile was fading fast.

Three

"*Jace?*" Celie said his name, disbelieving, her voice soundless in the tumult of the lounge.

She truly didn't believe it. Jace Tucker? *Here?* Celie felt as if she'd been punched in the gut.

She closed her eyes for a moment, certain she had to be hallucinating, certain that the wholly incongruous cowboy hat she'd glimpsed across the room, which had drawn her like a moth to a candle, would vanish and her momentary twinge of homesickness would not have turned into a nightmare.

A cowboy on a cruise? she'd thought, smiling when she'd spotted the Stetson, unable to stop her feet moving in its direction. Seeing it brought so many memories of home.

Home. Not Jace. It couldn't be Jace Tucker! It just couldn't!

Her mouth was dry. Her palms were damp. Her heart

was playing leapfrog with her stomach. Celie squeezed her eyes shut, willing the hallucination to vanish.

But when she opened them again, Jace was still there. And if he'd looked astonished, too, at first, and had blinked and swallowed at the sight of her, now he was grinning. Of course he was grinning—the same crooked, teasing grin with which he'd baited her ever since he'd come back to Elmer.

"Well, Celie O'Meara, fancy meetin' you here," he drawled.

"Ooh, is this your friend, honey?" a soft female voice asked.

And Celie was suddenly aware of a wide-eyed blonde at Jace's right elbow looking at her eagerly. At his left elbow stood another blonde, looking equally interested. And, of course, since this was Jace, who obviously believed The More The Merrier, a third blonde, just fastening her life jacket straps, was looking her way, too.

Trust Jace, Celie thought, jaw tightening, to go on a cruise with *three* women!

Damn it to hell, she didn't see why he had to go on a cruise at all!

Especially *her* cruise!

"What are you doing here?" she demanded furiously.

All the blondes' eyes widened at her tone.

Jace's grin wavered just a little. And his body seemed momentarily to stiffen. But then he flexed broad shoulders, slouched slightly, lifted those shoulders in a negligent shrug and gave her an easy, lazy Jace Tucker smile. "Well, I came to see you, of course."

Celie felt as if steam were coming out of her ears. "Oh, of course you did," she spat.

If he had come intentionally—if his being here wasn't the most awful coincidence in the world—it was because

Jace Tucker was apparently willing to go to the ends of the earth to humiliate her.

He, of all people, knew what a failure she was. He knew Matt had dumped her. He probably even knew why, which was more than she did. Matt had probably spelled out all her failings in great detail.

And if that wasn't enough, he knew she'd spent ten years getting over it, refusing to date anyone else, dreaming about a movie star. He knew she'd bid her life's savings on a date with that star—only to have him turn around and marry her sister! Not that Sloan's marrying Polly had been a bad thing. It hadn't. And it hadn't hurt her, either.

But to anyone else hearing the story, she was sure she would sound like the most pathetic fool in the world. And she was sure Jace Tucker would be only too happy to share it.

Damn Jace Tucker! He knew every terrible secret she had—all the ones she'd put behind her, the ones she'd thought she'd overcome. She had made a new life for herself here. She wasn't The Girl Matt Williams Jilted here. She wasn't even The Woman Who'd Bid Her Life's Savings On Sloan Gallagher And Was Now His Sister-in-law.

No. She was Celie O'Meara, a bit of an innocent, perhaps, but still likable. She was a woman with a life. Not much of one yet, but it was improving. She had made friends. She had met men. Maybe not her perfect man yet…but she had hopes that she would, given time.

She wasn't stuck anymore. She was finding the confidence in herself to believe that she could pursue her dreams.

And now Jace was here—grinning, teasing, infuriating Jace—staring at her, *laughing* at her, undoubtedly finding her pathetic attempts amusing, and capable of ruining everything!

"Is this your girlfriend, Jace?" one of the blondes asked.

"The girl from back home?" said the second.

"Aren't you goin' to introduce us, honey?" said the third.

At their questions, Jace looked as startled as Celie felt. He also seemed to blush. Jace Tucker? Blush?

From embarrassment, no doubt, Celie thought, at the absurd idea that she could possibly be his girlfriend.

Not hardly.

Celie expected a prompt denial. But he just looked agitated and cleared his throat. "Um, this is, er...Celie," he said quickly.

They all beamed at her. "Hi, Celie!"

She blinked, surprised at their enthusiasm, but before she could ask the names of his harem, another voice cut in.

"You know zis man?" It was her boss, Simone, arching perfectly plucked eyebrows as she appeared next to one of the blondes and looked from Celie to Jace and back again. Her disapproval was obvious.

And there was no way to deny that she knew Jace now.

"He, um, used to work with me," Celie said. "That's all," she added firmly, because she knew how Simone felt about fraternizing between staff and guests.

Simone's brows arched even higher. "Zis man, he cuts ze hair?" She looked at Jace in disbelief from the top of his Stetson to the pointed toes of his cowboy boots. The blondes in Jace's harem looked equally astonished.

"No, he doesn't cut hair," Celie said hastily. "My other job. I worked in a hardware store back home, too." Not something she had put on her résumé. Her job at Artie's was something else she was quite sure Simone would look down her aristocratic nose at.

Simone, who made of point of telling everyone she had been "born in Paree," had very high standards. She believed in Sophistication, with a capital S and Elegance, with a capital *E*. She believed all her stylists should look like Paris models.

"You zink ze guests trust you to make zem be-you-ti-ful when you look like ze frump?" she'd demanded when Celie had shown up for work the first week with her hair in a smooth, unsophisticated style.

While Simone wanted her stylists for their skills first and foremost, she wouldn't take anyone who didn't have "ze potential." To look beautiful, too, she meant.

Celie, while always doing her best with what she had, had never considered herself beautiful. What Simone saw she wasn't sure, but from the amount of work Simone and the other stylists had expended on her, she was pretty sure her boss considered her a reclamation project.

The first day she arrived Simone had demanded that Stevie, the top stylist, cut her hair. "We bring out ze cheekbones, yes?" she said, and Stevie, nodding, had cropped Celie's dark hair in a short, feathery cut.

Amazingly it had brought out her cheekbones. Then Birgit, who was the closest thing to a makeup artist Celie had ever met, had been deputized to show her how to "make ze most" of what she had. With the deft use of liner and shadow and just a hint of blush on "ze cheekbones," Birgit had made her look almost elegant.

At least Celie had dared to feel elegant then. Now she felt like nothing so much as a fraud—an imposter—a country bumpkin trying to pass herself off as an urbane sophisticate.

And she was sure Jace Tucker could tell.

There was more than a hint of a blush on Celie's cheekbones now. She would have liked to drop right through the deck.

"Is no time for socializing now," Simone decreed. "You will get back to work." It was an order, and Celie knew it. And even though at the moment her "work" was supposed to be helping the passengers, she knew what Simone meant. Leave. Go up to the salon. Do not flirt with the passengers.

As if! Celie thought.

The last person in the world she would flirt with would be Jace Flaming Tucker. But she wasn't going to say so. And she was going to take advantage of the out Simone had given her.

"Of course," she said brightly to Simone. "I'm on my way."

Then she turned her best, polite-cruise-ship smile on Jace and his harem, trying to mask her panic as she said cheerfully, "Welcome aboard."

So much for inspiration.

So much for seeing Celie again and being the easy, teasing guy he was with every other woman. So much for knowing exactly what to say.

Cripes, he was lucky he'd managed to say anything!

Jace hunched on a bar stool, downing his fourth—or was it fifth?—whiskey of the evening, feeling the burn all the way to his toes and wishing that instead of feeling it, the booze would send him straight to oblivion.

God, what an idiot he was! He'd heard her voice, turned around, and had had his breath taken away.

Far from knowing what to say, he'd simply stood there, like a fence post, staring at Celie as if he'd never seen her before.

Well, he hadn't! Not like that!

He'd expected to see the Celie he knew, the quiet demure wallflower Celie. The sweet, self-effacing Celie. The Celie who had been in the background of life in Elmer as long as he could remember.

Sure, he'd always known she was pretty, but it had been

a quiet sort of pretty, a gentle, soft sort of pretty. It had never called attention to itself before.

Not like this!

This Celie was almost exotic—with huge eyes and sooty dark lashes, a Celie whose soft curly hairstyle had been exchanged for a snazzy funky layered look, a Celie with cheekbones!

Where the hell had she got those cheekbones?

Polly had always been the one with the cheekbones in the family. And you noticed because Polly had always had a thousand freckles which had called attention to them. Celie, on the other hand, had had the peaches-and-cream unblemished look. And damn it, her face had always been *round!*

Now she looked as if she'd been sculpted! As if some hotshot sculptor had taken her and discovered not just the curves, but the bones within.

Jace's mouth had flapped while he'd tried to think of something to say. That had been bad. Worse had been knowing she wasn't at all glad to see him.

He'd been afraid of that. But he'd dared to hope that maybe a little homesickness would have made her look on him as a friendly face.

Fat chance.

He felt—along with the whiskey—a hollow, desperate feeling deep in the pit of his stomach. What the hell was he going to do?

All around him people were having the time of their lives. They were laughing and talking, getting to know each other. They'd just had the first of what promised to be the most incredible bunch of meals he'd ever seen—which everyone else had relished and he'd gagged on.

"Are you feeling a little seasick?" Mary Lou had asked him sympathetically as he'd pushed lobster around his plate.

He'd shaken his head. It wasn't the sea that had made him sick.

"I always feel that way the first night out," Lisa confided. "Getting my sea legs takes me a day or so. You'll feel better tomorrow."

Jace had nodded and tried to eat. He'd tried to look like he was enjoying himself.

"I think it's his girlfriend," Deb said.

He'd been attempting to crack a lobster tail and, not exactly adept, he'd managed to make it skid off his plate.

Deb had just nodded triumphantly. "I'm right, aren't I?" she'd queried. "She's worrying you."

"She's not worrying me." Jace debated going after the lobster on the floor and decided he'd look even worse scrabbling around down there.

"Of course she's not," Mary Lou came to his defense like a mother bear whose cub needed protecting. "She was just surprised. And with her boss looking over her shoulder, I'm sure she had to try to appear indifferent."

"As long as she wasn't indifferent," Deb said with just a hint of ominousness in her tone.

"Of course she wasn't indifferent." Mary Lou huffed, looking offended on Jace's behalf. Then she gave him an encouraging smile. "I'd bet she was thrilled down to her toes. Goodness knows, I would have been. Land sakes, it isn't every day a man goes halfway across the world chasing the girl he loves."

Which made him feel like an even bigger idiot than ever.

"She'll come around. You'll see," Lisa assured him. "She'll just have to bide her time."

"Yeah." He hadn't thought about that. Just what he needed—another obstacle.

"Cheer up," they'd encouraged him. "Come to the show with us. Enjoy. Have a good time."

"Maybe when you get to your room tonight she'll be waiting for you," Lisa said brightly.

Maybe she would be.

But Jace didn't think so. And he was in no hurry to get there and find out. He hadn't gone to the show with Lisa, Mary Lou and Deb. He knew he couldn't sit through anything like that. He'd be too antsy. And when he tried sitting still for any length of time every rodeo injury he'd ever had came back to haunt him. He didn't need an evening full of aches and pains to go with the mess that his brain was already working up to.

He'd said thanks, but he thought he'd just hang around the sports bar, maybe watch a baseball game. He wondered if they had a pool table. He could pretend he was back at the Dew Drop in Elmer.

Artie would be rolling his eyes in despair.

Artie and his great ideas. Huh!

"How ya gonna know if ya don't even try?" he'd said again and again when Jace had waffled about going on the cruise. "She might just be bowled right over," Artie had said with a happy anticipatory grin. "Might throw her arms right around you."

Or wrap her fingers right around his neck and squeeze, Jace thought.

He sighed and signaled to the bartender for another whiskey.

Celie *never* called home from the ship.

From the very start she'd told herself she wouldn't do it. It was a matter of maturity. She was a grown-up, an adult. She didn't need hand holding anymore. She could manage on her own.

For thirty years she'd depended on her family—on her mother, but mostly on her oldest sister, Polly, to give her moral support, an arm to lean on, a shoulder to cry on. She'd been determined to stop.

So when Simone had yelled at her, when a passenger got upset with her, when Armand laughed at her and Carlos tried French kissing her and Yiannis's hands had wandered where they definitely should not have been, Celie had solved her own problems. She had coped.

She wasn't coping with this—not with Jace Tucker on her cruise. Her fingers were shaking as she called Polly. She'd punched in the number three times, having made mistakes because she'd had to look up the number since Polly wasn't in Elmer anymore. She and the kids had moved to Sloan's ranch near Sand Gap as soon as school got out.

It was possible that Polly might not even know he was here. But then again she might.

She might even know *why* he was here.

Better yet, she might know what Celie should do about him.

So much for being grown-up. So much for being able to cope.

"Celie? What's wrong?" Polly demanded the moment she heard her sister's voice on the phone.

"Nothing," Celie said quickly, trying to assuage the worry in Polly's voice. "Nothing at all."

"Then why are you calling?"

"Can't I just call to be sociable?" Celie tried to sound casual, cheerful, the "new improved version of Celie O'Meara."

But Polly, of course, knew better. "You could, but you haven't, so why start now?"

Celie sighed. Still, she knew she could hardly blame Polly for her cynicism. She'd always been the one Celie had turned to in moments of disaster. She was the one who had held Celie while she'd wept buckets over Matt. She was the one who'd made the brisk announcement in church that "that skunk Matt Williams" had chickened out. She was also the one who had encouraged Celie to get her cosmetology license and set up her own salon. She was the one who had urged Celie to get on with her life. And when Celie had, years later, finally got up the gumption to do it—and had bid on Sloan—Polly hadn't once said she was in love with him. She'd buried her own desires and had simply cheered Celie on.

Polly was the kindest, wisest, most wonderful sister in the world. But she, too, had a life these days Celie reminded herself. She didn't need to be bothered with her sister's woes.

"No, really," she said. "It's not a big deal." Celie tried backpedaling a bit.

But Polly was having none of it. "What isn't? You might as well tell me."

And Celie knew that was true. Once alerted to a problem, Polly didn't rest until she'd solved it. Celie sighed. "Jace."

"Jace? Something happened to Jace?"

"Nothing's happened to Jace. Yet."

"But…" Polly's voice died out. But before it did, it had sounded mystified.

"He's here!"

"Here? Here where? Where are you? In Elmer?"

"No! He's here on the boat!"

There was a moment's astonished silence. Then an intake and a slow exhalation of breath. And when she did speak it was a soft murmur. "Well, I'll be damned."

"You're not the one who's going to be damned," Celie muttered. "If he says one word about Matt, about Sloan, about the auction, about…*anything,* I'll kill him!"

"He won't," Polly said soothingly.

"How do you know he won't?" Celie was raking one

hand through her hair and strangling the telephone with the other. "What did he come for if not to make trouble?"

Polly started to say something, then hesitated. "Maybe you should ask him."

"I did ask him!"

"And what did he say?"

"He said—" What had he said? Celie tried to remember, but she'd been so aghast at the sight of him it took her a moment to reconstruct the conversation in her mind. And then all she could report was, "He said he'd come to see me!"

"He didn't say I've come to ruin your life?" Polly asked.

"He didn't have to say it," Celie grumbled. "What's he doing here?"

"He came to see you," Polly repeated what Jace had said. "Maybe he missed you."

Celie snorted. "Because there's no one else in Elmer he enjoys annoying half so much?"

"Possibly. Maybe he wondered what you were doing."

"He could have asked Artie."

"Maybe he did. Maybe he got curious and decided to see for himself."

"Maybe, maybe, maybe…"

Polly could go right on spouting maybes forever, Celie thought. They weren't convincing.

"Never mind," Celie said. "The real question is, what am I going to do about him?"

"Well, you could throw your arms around him and kiss him," Polly said dryly, "but somehow I suspect you've already rejected that notion."

Celie shuddered at the very thought. "No way. I want to stay as far away from Jace Tucker as possible."

Again Polly hesitated. Then she ventured, "Didn't you

ever hear the saying about the best defense being a good offense?''

''I never played football,'' Celie reminded her. She had not been the tomboy in the family. But even though she hadn't, she suspected she knew what Polly was getting at. ''You want me to be nice to him.''

''Well, I should think that would go without saying,'' Polly said tartly. ''I was thinking you might go a little further.''

''Throw my arms around him and kiss him?'' Celie could barely get the words out of her mouth.

''It would definitely give him a shock.'' Polly laughed.

But Celie wasn't about to do that. She shouldn't have called Polly, either. Her sister was newly and happily married. She couldn't be expected to come up with ways to deal with a pain in the neck like Jace. ''Forget him. Forget I mentioned him,'' she said firmly. ''Tell me about the kids, about Sloan.''

It was a measure of how happy Polly was that she did precisely that. In the old days, after her husband Lew had been killed and before Sloan had appeared in her life, Polly had never just rattled on cheerfully about her life. She was too busy coping to sit back and reflect on it.

But tonight she did. She told Celie about the kids—about Jack's new puppy and the play that Lizzie was writing and the horse that Sloan was helping Daisy to train. She talked enthusiastically about having Sloan home for another month this summer before he had to go to Mexico to begin making his next film.

She even seemed philosophical about her oldest daughter, Sara. ''She's doing all right,'' Polly said now. ''Coping. Far better than I thought she would.''

Sara, a student at Montana State, had set her sights on medical school at an early age. She'd bought a day planner when she was in sixth grade, and she'd never settled for a

B when an A was a possibility. Her life had always been planned out five years into the future.

Until last February.

In February Sara had met Flynn Murray, a reporter who'd come to cover the auction as a bit of weird western local color for the offbeat New York based magazine, *Incite*. One look at Flynn, and Sara's well-ordered life had gone spinning out of control.

Just how far out of control no one, not even Sara, realized at the time.

Four weeks later with the auction long over and Flynn long gone, she did. Goal-oriented, schedule-bound Sara was pregnant with a child who fitted into neither her schedule or her long-term plans.

It must have devastated her, Celie thought, but she'd never said a word.

Not until May on the eve of their leaving for Hawaii so Polly could marry Sloan, did she end up having to tell. The stress of the past months had taken their toll and she'd nearly lost the baby. She'd lost weight, lost sleep, begun bleeding.

That was when Polly had found out.

It hadn't been an easy time for any of them. Polly had called off the wedding and had taken Sara to the hospital. She'd sat by her daughter's bedside day and night. Sloan had come flying home from Hawaii, worried about Sara but frantic that Polly meant to call the wedding off forever—which she had.

Polly—ever-capable Polly—had finally reached her limit. She'd raised four kids almost single-handedly for the past six years. She'd salvaged Celie from depression after Matt; she'd helped their other sister, Mary Beth, through her pregnancy with triplets; she'd been the tower of strength for her mother when their dad had died. And she hadn't even known her own daughter was pregnant!

She had failed. That's what she'd told Celie in the middle of the night as they'd paced together outside Sara's hospital room.

"No, you haven't!" Celie had argued. "You're always there for everyone. Now it's time to let Sloan be there for you."

But Polly wouldn't do it. She couldn't, she admitted. She was afraid to.

In the end it was Sara who'd made her mother see reason. It was Sara, home from the hospital, pregnant and determined to have this baby and see what life brought her, who took her mother to task.

Polly, her daughter had told her, was the one who had taught them all that life and love were worth taking risks for. That was why she'd loved Flynn, she'd told her mother.

"As if it were my fault she got pregnant," Polly had muttered later to Celie. But there had been color in her cheeks again. She had looked like Polly again, stubborn and determined, as she'd packed her suitcase to go to Hawaii to face Sloan, to tell him she loved him, that she was ready to take a risk.

Between Polly and Sara—not to mention her mother who, marrying Walt Blasingame last month, had taken some risks herself—Celie had had plenty of role models. It was because of their influence that she'd dared take this job in the first place.

And now, as she thought about it, her resolve returned. She stood up straighter. She took a deep breath. "Thanks, Pol'," she said.

"Thanks? For what?"

"For everything," Celie said. "For being there."

"Are you all right, Cel'?" Polly asked worriedly.

"I'm fine. I'll be fine," Celie assured her. She hung up and squared her shoulders.

She could deal with Jace Tucker.

* * *

The phone's shrill ring jarred Jace to semiconsciousness. He groaned, eyes closed and yanked the pillow over his head. Artie could answer it.

It rang again.

C'mon, Artie.

And again.

Annoyed, Jace rolled over and felt as if Noah Tanner had turned out a herd of bucking horses inside his head. "Artie!" He tried yelling, in case the old man didn't hear it, but then he realized the old man wasn't going to hear it—he was a couple of thousand miles away.

And the phone ringing by his bedside was the cell phone he'd agreed to take along so Artie could call him in case of "emergencies," though what emergency he could possibly do anything about from the deck of a ship miles away, Jace had no idea.

Hell's bells, had the old man had another heart attack?

Disregarding the pounding in his head, Jace pried his eyelids open, grimaced at the little light filtering around the heavy drapes into the room, and reached for the phone. *"What?"*

"Took ya long enough," Artie said cheerfully. "Does that mean you ain't alone?"

"Wha-what are you talking about?" Jace tried to sit up, got kicked in the head by all those horses inside and carefully lay back down again. "What's wrong?" he asked, trying not to raise his voice.

"Nothin'. Here." Pause. "How're things there?"

"Things are…all right." That was about the best he could say. And it was the truth, if he lay absolutely still and didn't even move his mouth very much. The horses in his head were just trotting now, but they still made even his teeth hurt. Why the hell had he drunk so much whiskey?

"Seen Celie?"

Oh, yeah. Jace remembered now why he'd drunk so much whiskey. He didn't answer Artie. "What's the emergency?"

"Told ya. Ain't none. 'Cept I ain't slept for worryin' about you."

"Well, stop worrying about me," Jace said through his teeth.

"Can't," Artie said matter-of-factly. "Lessen you can give me a reason to—like you proposed already an' Celie said yes." There was so much hope in his voice that Jace's teeth came together with a snap.

His head very nearly exploded. All the horses bucked at once. And the pain was so fierce it robbed him of breath.

"Ah, well, I figured it'd be too much to hope for," Artie said in the silence that followed. "But ya did see her." It wasn't a question, but it came close.

"I saw her," Jace managed at last.

"She glad to see ya?" Artie asked eagerly.

"Thrilled. Threw her arms right around me. Gave me a great smackin' kiss," Jace said dryly.

"Knew it!" Artie chortled happily, then suddenly stopped. "Yer havin' me on," he accused. "What did she do? Really."

"She looked like she wanted to throw acid in my face. This wasn't a good idea, Artie."

"Huh." The old man snorted. Then he paused. "Don't be a quitter. It's just gonna take some doin' is all."

Jace would have rolled his eyes, but he figured it might set the horses to bucking again. "Uh-huh."

"Don't worry. She's just playin' hard to get."

"That's one way of describin' it."

"So you gotta do the same."

Jace groaned. "Artie, you're nuts. I'm *here,* for cryin' out loud. I'm stuck on this blinkin' ship for a week. How hard to get can I possibly be?"

"Well…" Artie considered that.

Jace regretted once again letting the old man talk him into the cell phone. "Artie, this is not an emergency."

"Sez you." Artie sighed. "So if you ain't gonna sweep her off her feet, and you don't want to play hard to get, what're you gonna do?"

"Enjoy the cruise."

Artie groaned. "You are a quitter."

"I am *not* a quitter! I'm just…bidin' my time."

"Uh-huh." Scepticism dripped from the word.

"Lettin' her get used to me bein' around."

"Right."

"I'm serious. I think she's afraid of me."

"Yup. Terrifyin', that's you."

"C'mon, man, gimme some moral support here!" Agitated, Jace started to sit up. The horses kicked him in the head again. He groaned and lay back down.

There was a long moment's silence. Finally Artie said, "Okay, here's your moral support. I believe you ain't as big an idiot as you're actin'. But goldarnit, Tucker, you're comin' close!"

Celie waited all the next day for the other shoe to drop—for Jace Tucker to show up, for word to drift down about her being jilted, about her bidding on Sloan Gallagher, about what a sorry sad woman she really was.

But she didn't hear a word.

She worked an incredibly long day—starting before eight in the morning and finishing up after eight that night because it was a sea day. The first formal dinner would be held that night, and half the women on the ship wanted their hair fixed. They all talked and chatted and gossiped about everything under the sun.

But she never heard a word about herself.

And she never saw Jace, either.

She could almost have believed she'd dreamed him, but Simone came up to her when she'd been leaving that evening and buttonholed her as she headed for the door. "Zat man—zat *cowboy*—who come on ze ship, he is your lover?"

"No!"

Simone's very expressive brows did their disbelieving arch. "No? But he say he comes to see you."

"To annoy me." How could she possibly explain the very antagonistic relationship she had with Jace? "I'm sure he was as surprised to see me as I was to see him."

"He did not know you were here?"

Celie wetted her lips. "I...don't know."

"Hmm." Simone tapped a bloodred fingernail thoughtfully on her chin. "We shall see," she said after a moment's consideration. Her gaze leveled on Celie. "You know ze rules."

"Yes."

Simone nodded. "We charm ze guests. We have a drink wiz ze guests. We don't sleep wiz ze guests." She came down on this last with both feet in hobnailed boots.

"Of course not!"

"And you will remember." It wasn't a question. It was an order.

As if she needed one.

Remember not to sleep with Jace Tucker? Celie wouldn't have any trouble at all remembering not to do that!

Four

Jace spent most of the morning in bed, nursing his hangover and resolving, regardless of the provocation, to leave whiskey alone for the rest of the cruise. Hangovers, he discovered, were bad enough on dry land. On a ship, where the floor tipped and swayed, they were close to fatal.

He couldn't manage breakfast. The very thought turned him green. So he turned down Lisa and Deb and Mary Lou's invitation to join them. He didn't even bother to open the door.

"I'm gonna sleep in awhile," he told them as loudly as he dared. A certain decibel level caused his head to threaten to fall off.

"You do that, sugar," one of them called back cheerfully. "We'll stop by later."

Take your time, Jace thought. But he didn't say it. He just carefully—*very* carefully—rolled over and tried to go back to sleep.

He must have done it because the next thing he knew he was awakened by more knocking on the door.

"Jace? You all right, sugar? Feelin' better now?"

"F-fine," he croaked. "'M fine." He winced and slowly levered himself up. His head hurt, but the horses weren't bucking so hard anymore—and the room wasn't spinning quite so fast. In fact, as he got his bearings, it slowed and stopped.

"Great! You can come to lunch, then."

Lunch? It didn't sound as repulsive as breakfast had. He didn't feel nauseated anymore. His stomach actually rumbled. Slowly he hauled himself to his feet. His brain still felt a little too large for his skull.

"It's what comes of picklin' it," Artie would have said.

Jace didn't want to think about Artie.

"If you don't feel well enough," one of the blondes outside his door called, "we could send for the doctor."

"No! I mean, no. I'm…fine. Like I said."

"So you want to come to lunch? We're going swimming this afternoon. You could come along."

"Er," Jace wasn't sure he was up to swimming. But then, he thought, he had to do something. If he didn't, the whole cruise would be over and he'd have nothing to show for it—not even a tan!

"Yeah. Okay. Gimme twenty minutes. I gotta grab a shower."

It took him half an hour. He showered. He shaved. He studied his sunken bloodshot eyes and told himself to get a grip. He wasn't going to let Celie drive him to drink. He wasn't going to let Celie drive him crazy. He was going to act like a sensible, honest-to-goodness adult.

He could just imagine Artie rolling his eyes.

"Yeah," he said to his reflection in the mirror, "but Artie doesn't have any better ideas."

* * *

He went to lunch with Lisa, Mary Lou and Deb. He was a little shaky and a little pasty-faced, and his stomach recoiled at the thought of some of the dishes he was offered. But he did manage to eat a reasonable lunch. And he managed to find his sense of humor and the dregs of his usual charm, and after lunch he went on deck with them to check out the swimming pools, and before long not only were Lisa and Mary Lou and Deb smiling and laughing with him, but half a dozen other women were smiling and laughing and chatting with him, as well.

"We don't often see a cowboy on a cruise," some of them said to him.

And Jace quite frankly said that most cowboys really didn't have time to go on cruises, and when they asked him to explain what it was that cowboys—real cowboys—did all day, he sat down on a deck chair by the pool and held forth.

He talked about rodeo cowboys and then about regular ranch hand cowboys. They listened avidly, as if they were amazed such creatures still existed.

"It's like something out of a movie," one of the women said. "Like Sloan Gallagher's latest."

Jace grinned. "Oh, not really, ma'am. On film Sloan's a little too neat and clean. Not like real life at all."

"You know Sloan in real life?" another woman asked.

And Jace said he did.

"Ohmigod, he knows Sloan Gallagher!"

The cluster of women by then had reached more than a dozen. "Tell us about Sloan," they clamored. "Tell us more about cowboying."

Jace did. He told them his best Sloan Gallagher story— the one where they'd got into a fight as teenagers and he'd broken Sloan's nose. Then, because he played fair, Jace told them about their next battle where Sloan had broken his, as well.

"We sort of declared a truce after that," he said. "An' then he moved away."

"He's from Montana, though, isn't he?" a pert redhead asked.

Jace nodded.

"From that funny little town that had the auction last Valentine's day," a brunette remembered. "Wilmer?"

"Elmore?" a blonde suggested.

"Elmer," Jace said.

More women joined the crowd. "Tell us about Elmer."

So he told them about Elmer. Most of them knew a little bit. They'd all read articles about it. They had all seen Polly on television.

"The postmistress." They all nodded and beamed, remembering Polly's fifteen minutes of fame. "She was wonderful. So sane. So sensible. So strong. Do you know her?" they demanded.

Jace said he did.

"What's she like?" an older woman asked him. "She married Sloan, didn't she?"

"After her sister won him in the auction!" the redhead said.

"Talk about sibling rivalry! Wonder what her sister thought of that!" The women tittered.

Jace didn't say, *You could always ask her.*

Celie obviously hadn't claimed the fame of having spent a weekend with Sloan Gallagher. And she wouldn't thank Jace for mentioning it, either. So he answered their questions about Elmer, about Sloan and Polly in general terms, and he didn't mention Celie by name at all.

"It sounds wonderful." Several of them looked dreamy-eyed at the notion of packing up their lives and moving to Elmer.

"Maybe we should have done that instead of having come on the cruise," one mused.

"Maybe you should," Jace said, feeling like a member of the chamber of commerce.

"Maybe we will," said the redhead. "How many unattached cowboys would you say there are?"

Jace's brows lifted. All the women were looking at him expectantly. He scratched his head and tried to tick over all the guys he could think of. If he counted all the ones who came out of the woodwork to attend Noah and Taggart's bronc and bull-riding school there were quite a few.

When he said so, they crowded in closer. "Bull and bronc riders?" they said eagerly.

"Like you?" asked a woman who had just joined the group.

"I was," he said. "Not anymore. I'm done."

"Aw." Several of them looked sad on his behalf.

"Why are you quitting?" the redhead asked.

"Doc said I oughta find another line of work. Got in a pretty bad wreck at the finals last year. Broke my leg in two places. Got concussed."

The women all winced. One patted his jeans-clad leg gently. "Poor Jace."

"I'm all right now." He wasn't interested in sympathy. "I'm ready to move on, do somethin' else." And if he hadn't been sure of it last January, he was now. He liked being back in Elmer. He just wanted Celie there with him.

"I'm ready to settle down."

Every pair of female eyes widened. Several women's mouths formed small round *o*'s. There were murmurs and mumbles. The women all looked at each other, then every one of them looked at him.

Cripes, didn't they believe him?

Was the whole world made up of Celie O'Meara clones?

"I am," Jace insisted. "I'm done travelin'. I'm diggin' in back in Elmer, settlin' down, puttin' down roots."

Still they stared. One or two even blinked their disbelief. "I want to get married," Jace said firmly.

"Just ask me," one of the women in the back said.

They all laughed.

And Jace laughed, too, albeit a little grimly. "I already got the woman picked out," he told them.

"She works here," Lisa said.

"On this ship," chimed in Mary Lou.

"Who is she?" a chorus demanded.

"Yeah, just tell us and we'll knock her off," said the one in the back.

They all laughed again.

Then the older woman patted his hand. "She's a lucky lady, dear."

Jace wondered if she'd like to tell Celie that.

"Have you seen the cowboy?" Celie's first appointment asked her the following morning. It was the second full day of the current cruise and they had docked at Nassau early this morning. Only Celie and Stevie were working in the salon, the rest of the staff taking advantage of a day in port to go ashore, like most of the passengers.

The staff rotated working on-shore days, and since Celie had been in Nassua several times already, she was quite happy to work this shift. She told herself she'd rather be here than out wandering around the straw market or sunning on the beach where she might run into Jace Tucker.

She hadn't seen him since the first night. And even after Simone's little lecture about "not sleeping wiz ze passengers," she had begun to think she'd hallucinated the whole thing.

But now the pixyish redhead whose hair she was shampooing made her stop in her tracks.

"Cowboy?" Celie echoed carefully.

"Mmm." It was a very appreciative mmm. "What a

hunk. I never thought I'd say it…I'm a city girl myself," the redhead confided, "but he can put his boots under my bed anytime."

"Did he offer?" Celie asked before she could stop herself. "I mean…" she began, but the redhead cut her off.

"Don't I wish." The redhead sighed.

Half an hour later Celie's next appointment asked almost the same question. "Did you meet the cowboy?"

They couldn't all mean the *same* cowboy, could they?

"The cowboy? Is he a stage act?" There were plenty of entertainers on the ship. They changed periodically and she couldn't keep them all straight. Maybe the cowboy was a new one.

"No." This woman was sixty if she was a day, but her eyes lit up when she spoke. "Not this one. This one is the real thing!"

"The real thing?" Celie echoed, nerves really tingling now as she clipped away on the woman's hair.

"Oh, my, yes. I met him at the swimming pool yesterday afternoon. He was just the cutest thing in his jeans and his boots. And so polite. 'Yes, ma'am, no, ma'am.' Why, he could give lessons in proper behavior."

Give lessons on proper behavior? It couldn't have been Jace.

The next woman who came in had been there, too.

"Oh, yes, he's polite," she agreed. "And gorgeous, to boot. Dark-brown hair. Deep-blue eyes. And he said he knew Sloan Gallagher."

"He did?" Celie almost dropped the scissors.

The woman nodded. "Broke his nose, he said, when they were boys. And then—" she giggled "—he said Sloan turned right around and broke his!"

"Um," Celie said, mind whirling, fingers clenching on the scissors. "Is that…all he said?"

"He said he was settling down."

"What?" The scissors hit the ground with a clatter. "Oh, dear. I'm sorry. I—" Celie bent to pick them up and tried to regain her equilibrium at the same time.

After all, it wasn't entirely news. She'd heard that before—from Jace himself. He'd begun building a house on the ranch he owned with his sister and her husband to settle down in—at least that was what he'd told her months ago.

"Settle down? You?" she'd said snidely. Then she'd asked if he had someone in mind to share it with. She'd been shocked when he'd said yes. But since then he'd shown no signs of settling on one particular woman.

Maybe he wasn't planning on settling down with just one, she thought grimly. Maybe he was planning on settling down with a harem—like the three blondes he'd come to the safety demonstration with!

How very like him, Celie thought later as she scrubbed furiously at the hair of her next client. The woman winced, and Celie, realizing how fiercely her fingers were rubbing, stopped abruptly.

"Sorry," she apologized. "I just...get a little enthusiastic sometimes." All she needed was for the woman to complain to Simone.

"Wouldn't mind him settlin' down with me," that woman said with a smile, "but he says he's got someone in mind."

Celie didn't believe it. Not for a minute. If Jace Tucker had a woman in mind, she'd know it. She'd know *her!* There weren't that many women in Elmer and the surrounding valley.

If a guy was courting seriously, he'd never be able to keep it a secret.

Jace was just telling them a tale about this "someone" he was serious about, Celie decided, so they wouldn't any get ideas about roping him and tying him down.

What better way to make sure the women he wanted to

play with didn't take him seriously than to claim he already had a girlfriend?

The man ought to come with a warning label, she thought: Hankering After This Man Can Be Dangerous To Your Emotional Health.

All day long she was treated to the wonders of Jace Tucker. He was handsome, he was sweet, he was drop-dead gorgeous. He could braid horsehair bridles and play the guitar and he could dance the two-step.

The women seemed to be falling all over themselves talking about how great he was. Even Kelly, who ran the fitness center, came in singing his praises.

"Did you meet the cowboy yet?" she asked Celie, eyes shining. "He came in to use the whirlpool last night to help his leg. Poor guy, he got hurt in a rodeo accident."

Celie grunted. She didn't want to talk about Jace. She didn't want to hear about Jace. She didn't want her mind's eye to even attempt to imagine what Jace Tucker would look like sitting in a whirlpool.

She grunted and turned away, going back to the woman whose hair she was coloring. But the woman had been in the whirlpool with Jace.

He was, she said, "edible."

Celie did not want to think about it.

She didn't want to think about him—but she did. And as she did, she figured out finally why he'd come on the cruise.

It was an ideal place—a perfect place—to meet women.

Cruises attracted women, *lots* of women. Some married couples came on them. Relatively few single men did. Mostly there were just lots and lots of unattached women. Women looking for a little excitement, a shipboard romance, a one-week fling.

They were like buckle bunnies without the rodeo. Oh, not all of them, to be sure. But enough to keep Jace plenty busy. No wonder he'd booked a cruise. He couldn't rodeo anymore.

What better place for a babe magnet like Jace to have his pick of eager females, make a little whoopee and ride off into the sunset at the end of the week?

Celie, having listened over the past few weeks to more than one woman whose heart had been broken by just such a bounder, was incensed on behalf of all the foolish women he would be deceiving!

What's more, she felt responsible!

If Simone caught her prowling up here, Celie knew she—and her fledgling career as a shipboard hairstylist— would be toast.

Allison, her roommate, had told her to mind her own business. Stevie and Troy had said there was nothing wrong with having a good time with other passengers, for heaven's sake. They were all adults here, weren't they?

They were. But it didn't matter. Celie didn't know why it didn't matter—other than the fact that everyone knew Jace came from Elmer, which put Elmer's reputation on the line!

"What?" Stevie stared at her, disbelieving, when she said that.

"It's true!" Celie exclaimed. Jace Tucker was sullying Elmer's good name. And she was going to do something about it!

When she finished work, she lurked about waiting for the passengers to come back from Nassau, hoping to catch him then and have a word with him. But when she saw him, he was surrounded by a bevy of females. And when he went to the whirlpool, there were so many following him in he looked like the Pied Piper of Hamlin.

Kelly caught a glimpse of her and waved. "He's here!" she hissed in a loud whisper. "Wanta get a look?"

Celie shook her head fiercely. "No, I was just looking for, er, Allison."

She'd ducked back out, fretted and fumed, pacing the halls. Then, when Simone came by and gave her a steely look, she beat a hasty retreat down to the staff quarters. She didn't need Simone getting annoyed with her again.

She went back up at the end of the dinner hours. But Jace hadn't gone to the same place he'd gone last night. He must have gone to one of the buffets. Or maybe, she thought grimly, he was sharing a meal in some woman's room.

She prowled the sports bar and the lounge and didn't find him. She couldn't imagine Jace going to one of the singing and dancing shows that every cruise put on. But, just in case, she checked the crowds pouring out of the theater.

She didn't see him anywhere.

So there was no hope for it.

She just had to hope that Simone, whom she'd seen in one of the lounges with a tall, handsome investment banker from Toronto, would be too busy "socializing" to check up on the whereabouts of the junior members of her staff.

Then she would never notice that Celie O'Meara was where she had no business being—about to knock on a passenger's stateroom door.

"You'll be sorry," Allison warned. She'd followed Celie, talking furiously all the way, trying to dissuade her from interfering.

But Celie wasn't dissuaded.

And she wasn't going to be sorry. Jace was!

She thumped loudly on the door.

"Heaven help us," Allison muttered. "I'm gone." And she went skittering down the hall, leaving Celie by herself.

One second passed. Two. Five.

He wasn't there, Celie thought, unsure whether she was relieved or more annoyed than ever.

Then suddenly the handle rattled. The door opened.

And Jace, barefoot and bare-chested, clad only in faded jeans, braced an arm on the door and said, "Look, I'm really tired. I—*Celie!*" His eyes widened in shock.

It was all Celie needed. "I'm not at all surprised," she said scathingly. "All those women can wear a man out."

His jaw dropped. "What?"

"Women. The blondes. The redhead. The brunette. The girl whose hair I just colored. She's platinum now, by the way, in case you don't recognize her in the morning."

"What the hell are you talking about?"

"I figured out why you're here," she told him icily.

Jace blinked. He looked suddenly nervous. As well he might, Celie thought angrily.

His shoulders hunched. The movement drew her attention to them, and then, because she couldn't seem to help it, she noticed his chest, his abs. A vision of Jace in the whirlpool rippled unbidden to the surface of her mind. Furious at the direction of her thoughts, Celie shut her eyes.

"And I want you to stop."

He went rigid. Nothing moved but his adam's apple. He swallowed once, then again. "Stop?" He ran his tongue over his upper lip. "Stop what?"

"You know very well what! What you came for! Hitting on all these women!"

Jace's eyes widened fractionally. Then it seemed almost as if a small shudder ran through him. He flexed his shoulders, took a breath, then grinned a little. "Yeah, right."

"I mean it," Celie said, refusing to give in to the lethal Tucker charm. "I want you to stop it," she repeated.

"Okay."

"What do you mean, okay?" she asked suspiciously.

He shrugged. "I'll stop."

"Well, good. See that—" But before she could finish her sentence, she heard voices coming from the stairwell at the far end of the corridor, and a couple came around the corner—a man in a tux and a woman with a tinkling laugh and a French accent.

Oh, dear God! There was no help for it—Celie pushed past Jace straight into his stateroom. "Shut the door."

It was his turn to blink. "What?"

"Shut the door!"

Jace shut the door. Then he turned and leaned back against it, folded his arms across his bare chest and regarded her levelly. "What a good idea," he said.

"It is not. But Simone was coming down the hall. My boss," she explained.

A brow lifted. "Ze French woman?"

Celie made a face and nodded. "She's…particular."

"Ah." He was still looking at her, his expression unreadable. He was grinning, but there was something in his eyes she couldn't fathom. Nervously Celie moved to the far side of the room so that the bed was between them.

A mistake, she realized at once. They both stood looking at each other—and the bed. And even though Jace hadn't moved, it felt as if he was closing in on her. "Stop that," she commanded.

"Stop what?"

"Looking at me that way."

"What way?"

"Like you…like you…" But she couldn't say the words *want me.* It was ridiculous to think such things. It was the way Jace looked at every woman!

"What happened?" she asked. "Did you run out of women in Montana?"

"You could say that."

She snorted. "I might have known! Well, you needn't think you're going to score here."

"No?" The word was a soft growl.

"No," Celie said recklessly. "You don't belong here!"

"And you do?"

The quiet challenge made her stop and glare at him. "What do you mean by that?"

"We don't either of us belong here, do we?"

"I have a job here!"

"Only because you ran away."

"I did not!"

"Did so. You had a perfectly good job back in Elmer. You had a perfectly good life back in Elmer!"

"Oh, yes," Celie said scornfully. "Living with my mother and her new husband? Or maybe living with my sister and *her* new husband?"

She supposed she could have stayed in the house she'd shared with Polly's family and her mother after they'd each moved away, but she couldn't imagine it. It was a huge place. She'd have rattled around in it. And she'd have been lonelier than ever.

"You could get your own damn husband!" Jace's eyes flashed.

Stung, Celie retorted, "What do you think I'm trying to do?"

His jaw worked, and he shoved away from the door to pace into the room. "You didn't have to come all this way for that!"

"No? What was I supposed to do in Elmer?" Celie said scornfully. "Put a sign in the window—husband wanted? Or maybe I should have put an ad in the paper?"

Jace was glaring at her. "You could have looked around. Found a local guy."

"Right. Like Logan Reese maybe? Spence Adkins? Lots of temptation there. A convicted felon and a surly cop. No, thank you very much. They're not my type."

"Thank God," Jace growled. His chest was heaving and his eyes glittered fiercely.

Celie folded her arms across her chest and glowered back at him as he came to loom over her. "Who else is there? Artie?"

"Guess," he ground out. And before she could respond—before she could do anything!—Jace reached out and hauled her into his arms and fastened his lips to hers.

In her life Celie had, of course, been kissed. She'd been engaged, after all. She'd experienced the fervor of Matt's youthful fumbling passion. She'd tasted masculine desire.

Even after Matt had jilted her, she'd known it vicariously. She'd dreamed of Sloan Gallagher's kisses. And in the past few months she'd actually had a few brotherly ones from Sloan for real. They'd had potential. But they were nothing like the kisses he'd given Polly. Those had been intense. One of the things that had driven her to take this job was her desire to experience that intensity directed at her.

And now she did. She felt an intensity, a hunger, a need that rocked her. She felt the power of masculine desire, pure and simple. And very definitely directed at her.

By Jace Tucker?

On the verge of melting, instead Celie came to her senses. She jerked back, pressed her hands against his chest and shoved. Hard.

She stared at him, her heart hammering. "'G-guess'?" she gasped, looking around wildly. Her mind buzzed. Her blood roared.

"What on earth do you—" But she couldn't finish, could only stare, transfixed, into his fierce gaze.

"That's what I'm doing here, Celie," he said harshly, and his voice was as fierce and forbidding as his face.

Celie gaped, mind reeling.

Then, desperately she lurched past him and wrenched

open the door. She darted out into the hall and practically knocked down the couple walking by as she flew past them down the hall.

"Mademoiselle O'Meara!" the woman in the twosome called after her.

Oh, God! But there was no way on earth Celie was stopping now.

Five

He'd blown it. Big time.

Damn it all to hell! He *knew* Celie was skittish. He knew she had to be handled with kid gloves, had to be made to feel warm and loved and secure.

So what had he done?

He'd grabbed her, for heaven's sake! His kiss had been anything but warm and tender. It had been hungry, uncontrolled, desperate.

Like him, Jace thought grimly, wiping a palm down his face. And if that wasn't bad enough, he'd blurted out all that stuff about her finding a local guy for a husband, too, then telling her that's why he'd come!

Nothing like playing all your cards by simply throwing them at her face!

Of course, if she'd gone all starry-eyed and eager and said, "A local guy? Like you?" he might have been glad he'd done it.

But she hadn't. She'd been scathing in her dismissal of Spence and Logan—and she hadn't considered *him* a candidate at all. For a single instant while he was kissing her, he thought he'd felt her surrender, he thought she'd begun to kiss him back. And then she'd shoved him away and bolted from the room.

He'd wanted to run after her, to apologize, to take that terrified look off her face. But she'd run desperately down the hall away from him, practically trampling the couple in her way, and before he could move, he'd heard a shocked, "Mademoiselle O'Meara!"

It had stopped him dead.

Her boss, the French dragon, was staring, astonished, after her. And when Celie disappeared around the corner, the dragon turned and fixed him with a hard stare. It centered for a very long moment on his bare chest and then slowly, disconcertingly, traveled up to meet his eyes.

"Ah," she said, ice dripping, "the friend." It was amazing how much doubt and distrust the woman could get into one single word.

Jace bristled, then gathered his wits and forced himself to calm down. It didn't take a psychologist to know that Madame Dragon was ready to fire Celie. And it didn't take a conflict-resolution specialist to know that being the guy who got her fired would rank right up there with being the guy who'd called to tell her Matt wasn't marrying her.

Not in his best interests, to say the least.

He took a slow, careful breath. "That's right," he said. "We go back a long way, Celie and I. We grew up together, and I invited her to come see some pictures from home." He spoke matter-of-factly and hoped the dragon bought it.

"Pictures," she echoed, her gaze sliding down to his bare chest again. "Indeed?"

"Indeed," Jace said firmly. "She's been kind of homesick. Told her sister, and she told the old man I work for..." He shrugged, as if the conclusion ought to be self-evident. "Celie's a good kid. Kind of naive. But sweet." God, he couldn't believe he was saying this. "She spent her whole life in Elmer, you know. But she always wanted to see the world. It just took her a while to get up the gumption to do it. We're all real proud of her for goin' out and doin' this."

He was, in a perverse, annoyed sort of way damned proud of her. Taking this job, bidding on Sloan, going to Hollywood with him—drat her!—had all proved that Celie had more guts and gumption than he'd ever have guessed.

"So you come to check on her?" Fine dark brows arched skeptically over the dragon's dark eyes.

"Yeah. Her sister thought it would be nice if she saw somebody from home. And I sort of figured it was time for a vacation. So I said I'd come and see her. Kinda let her know we aren't so far away, after all. An' it worked," he said brightly. "She's cured."

"Cured?" The dragon brows arched even higher.

"Not lonely anymore," Jace said. "In fact she didn't even stay to see all the pictures. She noticed the time and jumped up just like that an' said she had to go." He gave the woman his most charming smile. "That's why she was runnin' out the door. She knew she had to get up and get to work early tomorrow. Real conscientious, that's our Celie."

"Mmm."

Whether the dragon believed a word he was saying he had no idea. But short of calling him a liar—and if staff weren't supposed to fraternize with passengers, they probably weren't supposed to call them liars, either—Jace knew there was little she could do but nod her head and, he hoped, forget whatever notions she had about causing Celie any more grief.

"Ah, yes, Celie is most conscientious." She dredged up a begrudging smile and politely bestowed it on Jace. "A hard worker. But she is, perhaps, as you say, a little too naive…a little too innocent." She fixed Jace was a knowing look. "Is not ze best zing to go to a gentleman's room."

It didn't seem the time to tell her that Celie didn't consider him a gentleman.

"We're friends," Jace said firmly. "Like I said. I came to give her some moral support, see she was okay."

"And now you have seen her. Yes? Then how do you say…mission accomplished? So, enough mission. Now Celie gets her work done."

It wasn't a question. Bright eyes nailed him where he stood.

Jace nodded. "Of course."

The dragon bent her head. "I am glad we agree. Is good for everyone, you understand, that Celie will not be coming to your room again." Her smile blinded him. She gave an encouraging nod.

Jace knew what she wanted him to say. "I understand."

The smile grew several megawatts brighter. "Zen we say good night, monsieur." And, hooking her arm through the crook of the arm of the suit accompanying her, the dragon gave him one last nod, then waltzed away down the corridor.

Jace went back in his room, shut the door and sagged against it. Had he done it? No, better question. *What* had he done?

My God, he'd kissed Celie O'Meara! He'd virtually told her he'd come to marry her. And she'd turned tail and run in the other direction.

The phone rang. He snatched it up.

"So," said Artie. "You makin' any progress?"

＊　＊　＊

The trouble with being on a boat, Celie thought, pacing the upper deck, whirling at the fantail and pacing back the way she had come, was that wherever you went, there you were.

On the boat.

With your thoughts jumbled, your wits scattered, your mouth still tingling from the hard press of Jace Tucker's lips.

She pressed her fingers against her own lips now and could still feel the sensation that had shocked her to her core. *Jace Tucker had kissed her?*

Jace Tucker didn't even like her!

Did he?

She would have said not. She had always thought not. She had always thought she was beneath his notice. Silly, dull Celie O'Meara was hardly the sort of girl to catch a guy like Jace Tucker's eye.

Or was she?

The thought sent a shiver right down her spine. She and Jace Tucker?

Good God.

She reached the bow end of the deck and stopped, clutching the railing and staring out into the inky velvet sky and tried to arrange her thoughts, tried to make sense of a world turned upside down, tried to think! She tried to be logical like her niece Sara.

Well, like her niece Sara used to be. Before Flynn.

Sara said logic had gone right out the window where Flynn was concerned. Trying to explain how she could have simply tossed her day planner and her common sense right out the window, she'd told Celie, "I don't know really. I felt some sort of primordial attraction I never even imagined existed until he walked into my life." She'd looked dazed. And then she'd said urgently, "Do you know what I mean?"

Celie hadn't. Now she suspected she did.

She'd felt an urge she'd certainly never experienced before, when Jace's lips had touched hers. She'd felt hot and hungry and eager and desperate. She'd wanted the kiss to go on and on and on. She'd wanted other things to go from there. She'd wanted…Jace!

She gave herself a little shake and began pacing again, mind still spinning, body flushed with desire and barely cooled by the late-night breeze that caressed her skin. She barely felt it. Just as she barely saw the sliver of moon in the black velvet sky or the stars scattered like diamonds across it.

Instead she saw Jace's face. She saw the way his blue eyes had glittered as he'd looked at her, the way his hard mouth had twisted when he'd said those words. *That's what I'm doing here.*

Those words. She ran them over and over in her mind. "You could get your own damn husband! You could have looked around. Found a local guy." And then, when she'd scornfully challenged him to name a local guy, he'd said just one word: "Guess." And then he'd kissed her.

And then she relived the kiss. She'd never been kissed like that. Had never known that hunger, that intensity, had never *responded* with equal need. She still felt weak at the knees and fuzzy between the ears.

"That's what I'm doing here, Celie." She could hear the harsh words now.

That's what I'm doing here.

She stopped pacing and stood absolutely still, letting the late night breeze hit her squarely in the face as she stared into the darkness and considered the meaning of those words.

He'd come to…to *court* her?

It seemed so unlikely she shook her head. It boggled her mind. It was so unlike Jace.

Wasn't it?

She tried to think. Jace Tucker wanted her. She tried out the notion. Bent her mind around it. Said the words.

"Jace Tucker wants me." She rolled his name around in her mouth, tasted it the way she had tasted his lips less than an hour before. Could still taste his lips now.

Jace Tucker wanted her.

No. He didn't simply *want* her. That wasn't what he'd said.

He wanted to *marry* her!

Well, he hadn't said that, either. Not in so many words. But that was what he'd meant, wasn't it? It was her finding a husband that they'd been talking about.

She tried saying, "Jace Tucker wants to marry me," out loud and couldn't. Her tongue seemed welded to the roof of her mouth. She gripped her hands together tightly, as if the pressure from them would push more blood up through her over-heated body into her befuddled brain, as if it would help her make sense of this astonishing notion.

He wanted to *marry* her?

No. He couldn't.

But if she put everything he had said together—and combined it with that kiss!—that was the total she got. She did the addition again—and again. Every time it came out the same way.

And she, ninny that she was, instead of asking him what he was talking about, instead of insisting he spell it out, had panicked and run!

"Jace Tucker wants to marry me?" She got the words out finally, but they came out a question. She couldn't quite say them matter-of-factly. Still she stood staring out into the distance and felt this incredible wave of…what? Peace? Joy? Satisfaction? Inevitability?…wash over her.

Inevitability?

Oh, Celie. She shook her head at her own idiotic notions.

The first gurgle welling up in her chest caught her by surprise, jolted her. But she couldn't swallow it, couldn't make it go away. And it spilled over. She giggled. She gurgled. She laughed. She could feel tears she laughed so hard.

It was preposterous. She and Jace Tucker. And yet…it wasn't.

She didn't believe it. And yet she wanted to.

And that surprised her, too.

She'd dreamed of finding the other half of her soul for as long as she could remember. She'd thought she'd found him with Matt. She'd dreamed foolishly that she'd found him in her fantasies of Sloan. Those, she'd begun to realize recently, had existed merely to keep her hopes alive. They hadn't been real. They hadn't been substantial. They'd simply been there—holding a place for the real man whenever he came along.

And was the real man Jace?

Did he love her?

Did she love him?

God knew she hadn't thought so. She'd hated him for years—even as she'd been fascinated by him.

Watching Jace had always been like staring into the sun—tantalizing and dangerous. His joy of life, his boundless enthusiasm, his easy way with people—especially his ability to charm the opposite sex—had always been a source of fascination. When Matt had gone down the road with him, she remembered listening eagerly to the tales he'd told about Jace. And Celie had been torn between her fascination and her very real fear that emulating Jace's lifestyle would not be conducive to Matt's getting happily married to her.

It turned out that she was right. And that was when her fascination had turned to resentment.

She had been convinced that Jace didn't think much of

her, either. He'd certainly gone out of his way to tease her, to bait her, to get in her way these last few months every time she'd turned around.

She'd thought he had been doing it to annoy her.

Now she didn't know what to think.

But she was intrigued. Astonished. Amazed.

He'd kissed her—very nearly melted her where she'd stood—and instead of seeing where things would lead, she had panicked and run.

She couldn't go back, either, she realized now. Because somewhere down there Simone was lurking—no doubt ready to fire her.

Oddly the possibility didn't make her knees knock. She would have expected to be gibbering with fear that Simone was going to sack her. But she wasn't. She wasn't even thinking about Simone.

She was thinking about Jace.

Something had quickened inside her at his kiss. Something had happened between them. It scared her and attracted her at the same time. The old Celie would have been crawling into a hole right about now. This Celie was intrigued. This Celie wanted to know more.

Tomorrow she would. They would sort it out, she and Jace.

They would talk tomorrow *after* she'd been fired. For the moment she would play it all over and over in her mind. She would taste his kiss and remember his words. *You could get your own damn husband. Find a local guy. That's what I'm doing here.* She knew she wouldn't sleep a wink tonight.

She didn't care.

Celie was up, waiting for Simone to rap on her door before seven. It had happened when she'd sacked Tracy. She'd turned up while Tracy was still in her nightclothes and had sent the other woman packing then and there. Celie expected the same.

"What are you doing?" Allison had squinted at her out of one bleary eye when Celie had got up at six. She hadn't slept at all, so it really hadn't mattered when she got dressed. It had been all she could do not to bounce off the walls. She wanted it over and done with. She wanted to go see Jace.

"I'm…restless," Celie said. She was tempted to tell Allison about last night, about Simone, about Jace. But she didn't want the entire ship gossiping about her. There would be plenty of that after Simone fired her.

So she sat on her bed, fully dressed, and waited. And waited. Allison dragged herself up finally, grumbling. She gave Celie an odd look, went to take a shower. When she came out Celie was still waiting.

"What are you doing?" Allison demanded.

Celie shrugged. She picked up the book she'd been holding in her lap. "It's a thriller."

Allison didn't look impressed. "If it's so thrilling how come you're on the same page you were when I went in to take a shower? Coming to breakfast?"

Celie shook her head. She didn't want to be at breakfast when Simone arrived. She might not care that she was getting sacked, but she didn't relish public dismissal. She nodded at the book. "I want to read this."

Allison shook her head. "Whatever." She waggled her fingers and went off to get a bite to eat.

By ten minutes to eight Simone hadn't come. She was obviously going to force Celie to come to work. So it would be a public dismissal in the salon. Celie squared her shoulders and went.

Simone was already there, picture-perfect in her pencil-thin black skirt and black silk shirt. She was chatting with two of the passengers, but looked up when Celie came in.

"A word wiz you, *s'il vous plaît*, Mademoiselle O'Meara." Her mouth, outlined in bloodred lipstick, formed the words as one long finger with an equally blood-red nail beckoned Celie into her office.

So the execution wouldn't be public after all. Celie was grateful.

"Come in. Shut ze door, mademoiselle."

Celie shut it. She took a deep, careful breath and let it out slowly. She would explain. She would be polite. And then she would be on her way. "About last night...Ms. Sabot. I went to—"

Simone cut her off. "I speak, mademoiselle. You listen."

Celie fell silent. The woman was, after all, still her boss, and Celie was always polite. She had also never been in a situation like this before. This must have been what it was like to be sent to the principal. The very notion of being so bad as to be referred to a higher authority had horrified her as a child. Now she simply waited for the inevitable and didn't really care.

"I speak wiz your friend," Simone began.

"My friend?"

"Ze man in ze room," Simone said patiently. "He explain why you were zere. He tells me he invite you to see pictures from home."

Celie stared, nonplussed. Jace had done what? She didn't speak.

Just as well because Simone went right on. "Of course, you understand zis is not so good." Simone shook her finger under Celie's nose. "Going to rooms of passengers is not recommended. You remember I say zat?"

"No, ma'am. Yes, ma'am." Three bags full, ma'am.

"But I understand homesick. Is a difficult zing to be homesick."

"Er, yes."

"You are new, Mademoiselle O'Meara. I understand you

can be homesick when you are new. You will not let zis happen again. Yes?'' Hard eyes bored into hers.

"Um…" Celie floundered.

"Yes," Simone answered her own question for Celie. "Ze answer is yes. You understand? So, good. Now is time to get to work." She gave a brisk nod, turned away and opened the door.

Celie didn't move. She stood stock-still, staring. She wasn't fired? Jace had lied and saved her job for her? And why had he done that? Her mind was doing somersaults again.

"And so, what do you wait for, zen, mademoiselle?" Simone tapped her pointy-toed shoe impatiently. "Your first appointment is waiting."

"Er, right." Celie hurried out past the older woman. She still had a job.

But what about Jace?

All day long Celie expected him to come to her.

It was a sea day. And the seas were somewhat rough because the wind had come up and there was a storm brewing. But though the ship rose and swayed, Celie remained steadfast at her post. The weather didn't bother her—and she wanted to be here when Jace came.

As long as she was here, he knew where she'd be.

She cut hair all morning, and though she kept one eye on the mirror as she clipped and snipped and shampooed and styled, Jace never came. In the afternoon she worked in the spa, giving massages. There was no mirror where she worked, and she had to crane her neck to see who came in. So making sure she saw him was a little more difficult.

"You remember my friend," she said to Allison and Stevie, "the guy from home? Well, if he comes in looking for me, let me know."

"You don't want us to tell him you're not here?" Allison said.

"No. I…I want to talk to him."

But the afternoon passed and Jace didn't come.

She didn't understand it. A guy didn't just blurt out things like Jace had and then vanish into thin air.

Except it seemed that Jace had. She worked until six o'clock. But he never came.

Lots of second thoughts did. They made her crazy. They caused her to question what she'd heard last night. Had she misinterpreted it? Misunderstood? She felt hot and then cold and then sick to her stomach.

But regardless of the words, there was no misinterpreting that kiss.

Was there?

Celie didn't see how. But she didn't see Jace, either.

Where was he?

"He never came in?" she said to Allison when they got off work.

Allison shook her head. "Never saw him. And—" she grinned "—believe me I looked. He's so gorgeous he'd be hard to miss."

"I know." It was one of the things that had always made him seem so daunting. When you got right down to it, he was every bit as good-looking as Sloan Gallagher. Far more gorgeous than she was, that was for sure.

Jace Tucker could have any woman he wanted. He couldn't really want her!

But every time she thought that, she thought about the kiss. She thought about his words. And she thought she had to know.

She would have to go to his room.

Simone breezed past on her way out the door and gave Celie an arch look, as if she had been reading her mind.

Celie took a deep, desperate breath and smiled brightly.

"Want to catch the film after dinner?" Allison asked as they left the salon.

"Not tonight. I need to…to do something."

"Oh, yes?" Allison slanted her a glance. "Going to read some more of that thriller?"

"What?"

Allison just laughed. "I thought so."

She didn't push any further, just grinned and said, "Good luck."

Celie figured she needed it. She felt wobbly and uncertain. All her insecurities came clamoring back. Maybe she should just forget the whole thing, pretend it hadn't happened.

Impossible. She couldn't.

She hadn't come this far to turn and run now. So what if she was mistaken? So what if she'd misinterpreted? She had to go see him, anyway, didn't she, to thank him for saving her job?

Yes, definitely. She had to do that.

She showered and changed her clothes, tossing the polo shirt and white denims that were her work uniform into her laundry bag and putting on a pair of dressy black slacks and a red silk shirt. It had been one of her first purchases after her first week's work, a bit of casual sophistication. Whenever she wore it she felt braver.

She needed to feel brave tonight.

Then she did her makeup, using every trick of the trade that Simone and Stevie and Birgit had taught her. War paint, Allison had called it once laughingly before she'd headed out on a date. Celie needed that tonight, too.

It was hard to do it well because the stormy weather was still rocking the boat, making her attempts at mascara and eyeshadow difficult. And she smeared her lipstick on the first attempt and had to scrub it off and start over. But finally she was ready.

Or not.

"Ready," she told herself firmly. She could do this.

But why hadn't he come? The thought niggled at her all the way to his room. It taunted her, worried her. It was making her crazy. Jace had always made her crazy.

Was it only twenty-four hours since she'd come to take him to task for attempting to seduce every woman on the ship? Oh, God. She stopped stock-still in the hallway, feeling equal parts panicky and foolish.

There was still time. She could turn around and go back to her room.

No, she couldn't.

At Sloan and Polly's reception she had danced one slow dance with Sloan. Once upon a time that would have been the stuff of dreams. It was very special even when he was Polly's husband.

But what made it most special of all was right at the end, when he had stopped and looked down into her eyes, his own gentle as he'd said, "It will happen to you, Celie. Believe it."

She knocked on Jace's door.

He didn't answer.

She shifted from one foot to the other, hyperventilating— her nerves jangling and fingers clenching as she waited. Far down the hall a couple came around the corner. *Please God, don't let it be Simone.*

It wasn't. The couple approached. Celie knocked again. They smiled at her as they passed. She jigged from one foot to the other and told herself she might as well leave, he wasn't there.

Of course he wasn't there. It was just past dinnertime. He was probably in one of the dining areas with the blondes. He was probably at the captain's table—he and the captain and eight of the ship's most gorgeous women.

He was probably in some woman's room right now—in bed. He was...

The door opened a crack, and Jace's unshaven face peered out. He took one look at her and groaned. "Oh, hell."

"What's wrong?" Celie demanded.

He looked awful. His dark hair was spiky and uncombed. His face was pale beneath his normal dark tan. He was wearing a T-shirt and a pair of jeans. It looked as if he'd dragged them on as they hung low on his hips and didn't seem to be completely zipped.

"Jace?"

"Go away." He started to shut the door.

She stuck her foot in.

"Damn it, Celie!" He pushed again, but she pushed against it and practically knocked him down as she went in.

"What's the matter with you?" she demanded as he glowered at her.

He looked around desperately, helplessly, then shrugged, took half a dozen steps and crashed facedown on his unmade bed again. "I'm seasick."

It was, Jace was sure, worse than being dead.

Dead sounded great. If he were dead, it would be over. He wouldn't be spending hour after hour enduring the most gut-wrenching, sweat-inducing, head-pounding experience of his life.

Boats! Cripes! Why had anyone ever invented them? If God had wanted men to float He would have made the sea flat. How the hell did people live like this?

Why had he come?

Celie. He'd come to win Celie. Artie had thought it would be a good idea. Jace wanted to kill Artie. Drowning would be too good for him.

He'd been moaning and tossing and turning for hours. He hadn't had a rational thought since sometime in the middle of last night. He'd lain awake most of it, worrying about what Celie must be thinking.

He'd known he would have to track her down first thing in the morning and tell her what he'd told her boss about her coming to see pictures in his room. She had to know he hadn't tried to get her fired.

And she had to know he wasn't trying to seduce her, either. Or take advantage of her. Which heaven only knew that kiss certainly could have implied.

That kiss. He'd tried to regret that kiss. He couldn't. He'd savored it.

But he knew he'd have to explain it, too—if she'd let him. He'd tried to figure out what he'd say. He'd muttered and paced and raked his fingers through his hair for hours. His head had begun to pound, his mind to reel.

He wasn't exactly sure when it was that he'd started feeling sick. Maybe it was when the floor began to shift sideways as he walked. Maybe it was when the lights seemed to sway. He got dizzy watching them and lay down so it would wear off.

It hadn't. And when he'd tried to get up again he could barely make it to the bathroom without losing his dinner. He made it. He lost his dinner. Things had gone downhill from there.

"Bit of a storm," the steward had said when he'd come to make up the room. He'd been smiling brightly. Jace had groaned and told him to go away.

The man had offered to bring him something to make him feel better. "Perk you right up," he said with considerable relish.

Jace had declined. The very thought of putting anything in his stomach had sent him staggering toward the bathroom again.

The steward had straightened up while he'd been in there. "You call when you want something," he'd said as he was leaving.

How about a funeral? Jace thought. It was the only thing that appealed.

He didn't get out of bed all day. The ship continued to rock. The lights continued to sway.

The blondes stopped to see if he wanted to come to lunch and dinner. He didn't. The understatement of the year.

"Want us to bring something back for you?" Deb asked, looking at him sympathetically as he clutched the door and tried to remain upright until they left. "There's something you can drink that's supposed to help."

"No." Jace didn't think he'd ever drink anything again, and he said so. They left with Deb muttering that he really should try. He stumbled back to bed again and wanted to die.

An hour later he heard knocking again. He didn't want to answer it. It would be Deb, undoubtedly, determined to force some awful medicine down his throat. He ignored the knocking. But it continued. She didn't go away.

He groaned. Damn it. Every knock pounded not just on the door, but in his head. "Okay, all right. I'm coming." Anything to get her to quit. He staggered up, stumbled across the room and wrenched open the door.

"Oh, hell."

He'd been horrified to see Celie standing there. God, no. He couldn't deal with her tonight. But he hadn't been quick enough to shut her out. And now he was lying facedown on the bed and she was standing over him.

"How long have you been like this?"

"Forever," he muttered into the sheet.

"Did you take anything for it?"

"No."

"You should. You'll be sicker if you don't. I'll go get something."

He tried to shake his head. A serious mistake. He hauled himself up and bolted for the bathroom, slamming the door behind him. A man needed a shred of dignity. He'd be damned if he'd let her in to play Florence Nightingale and hold his head for him.

Beyond the door Celie said, "I'll be right back."

He sank down and slumped against the wall of the bathroom and tried to muster the willpower to get up and go lock the door so she couldn't come right back.

He didn't make it.

"Drink this."

"No." Muffled into the sheet.

"Yes." She prodded his ribs.

Jace groaned. "Go away."

"No. I'm trying to help you."

"Shoot me."

"Sorry," she said with disgusting cheer. "No gun. Come on, Jace. I promise this will help. Truly. The bartender swears by it."

"The bartender?" He shuddered, remembering his hangover. He did not want to think about alcohol at a time like this. Bile rose in his throat.

"Nonalcoholic," Celie said, apparently able to read minds now. "Come on." She nudged him again.

Jace groaned and turned his head to eye her blearily. "If I drink it will you go away?"

She was looking down at him with those beautiful deep-blue eyes of hers and she shook her head solemnly. "Not a chance."

He shut his own eyes.

"We have to talk, Jace." Her voice was soft, tender, concerned, edged with worry. "About last night."

"I don't...didn't—" But he couldn't explain. Not now. Probably not ever.

He heard her swallow. She hesitated, then said quietly, "Didn't mean it?"

Something in her voice got to him. She sounded nervous, apprehensive. Doubtful. He opened his eyes and looked at her. The beautiful eyes were dark and serious, taking everything to heart. Jace pressed his mouth together in a thin line, drew a breath and nodded just slightly. "Meant it," he admitted.

Celie smiled then. It was like the sun coming out. It was her angel's smile. Sweet and pure and joyous. He'd seen it before—when she'd held a baby, when she'd come to see Artie at the hospital, when she'd kissed her mother and Walt at their wedding. He'd never seen it directed at him.

Her hand brushed lightly over his hair, and then cool fingers stroked his hot cheek. He very nearly moaned.

"Come on, Jace. Drink. You'll feel better." She held out the glass to him.

He struggled up and drank. It was vile. He gagged it down. Then he sank back against the pillows, spent.

"Satisfied?" he muttered when he could manage it.

Celie smiled and sat on the bed beside him, shaking her head as she did so. "Satisfied?" she echoed. "No, not quite yet."

Six

It was the weirdest dream he'd ever had.

He and Celie had been together in bed, their arms around each other. They were touching. Her hand had been stroking his hair. He thought she'd kissed him...before they'd slept.

He awoke dazed and disoriented, tangled in the bedclothes, straining to remember, to bring the dream back, to hang on to it for a few more minutes.

And then, slowly, as he looked around the room, he noticed that his head wasn't pounding anymore, that lights weren't swaying anymore and that there was an empty glass on the bedside table. And he realized that it might not have been a dream at all.

Celie had been here.

He rolled over, reached out. The other side of the bed was empty. But the pillow was crushed against the headboard, the blanket was rumpled. He rolled over and pressed his face to the pillow, inhaling deeply and groaning as he savored the soft fresh scent that was Celie.

Celie had been here.

And now she wasn't.

Why? He vaguely remembered her touching his cheek, smiling, saying. "Going to check in with Simone," she'd said. "Be right back."

How long ago had that been? He had no idea of the time, but beyond the drapes the sun looked high in the sky. It had to be late. And she wasn't back?

Why hadn't she come back?

Second thoughts? Had he done something unforgivable while he was asleep? He tried to think back, to dredge up more memories. The ones he did remember were embarrassing for the most part. He'd been sick as a dog all night, barely coherent, hardly in control. Pretty unforgivable. But she had stayed then. She'd stayed through it all.

She could have vanished right after she'd brought him that ghastly stuff to drink. She hadn't. Instead she'd climbed right onto the bed with him and let him put his head in her lap. And later, if he remembered right, he'd awakened once to find that she had slid down to lie beside him and they were wrapped in each other's arms.

He'd spent ten years imagining what it would be like to go to bed with Celie O'Meara. It had never been like that! Thank God.

And yet...

There had been something right about just lying with her, being with her. Something honest. Something real. Something he'd never experienced with any other woman.

"No kidding," he muttered gruffly. Celie was the first woman he'd ever only slept with—in the literal sense of the word.

Now he slowly eased himself to a sitting position and waited for disaster. But it didn't come. The room didn't rock. His stomach didn't roll. His mouth tasted foul, but he could solve that. He could brush his teeth, take a shower, clean up, get dressed.

And then he would go find Celie O'Meara—and they would talk.

"What do you mean I have to work?" Celie demanded.

Simone smiled unflappably and unrepentantly. "I'm so sorry," she said. "Stevie is sick. He cannot come in and of course Allison cannot do it all herself. Her schedule is full. Stevie has haircuts all morning and he was to do massage this afternoon. It's is a very good thing you, too, are qualified."

"But—"

But there was no *but*—and Celie knew it. There was only her job. And filling in when someone was sick was part of it.

Shore days were just like any other day if you were needed. Only today Celie hadn't intended to go ashore. She'd left Jace at the last possible minute, run back to her room, changed into the polo shirt and white jeans she wore when she was on duty and then run down to the salon. She expected to check in with Simone, grab a quick shower and run right back to Jace again.

"So you will start, now, yes." It wasn't a question. Simone was looking at her expectantly. She nodded at the woman who had just come into the salon. "Your first appointment is here."

Celie sighed. She took a deep breath. She hoped Jace understood. Then she pasted on her cruise-ship smile and beckoned the woman to her chair.

Allison was looking at her speculatively. "Missed you last night," she said. What she meant was *Where were you?*

Celie smiled. "Yes."

Allison's gaze narrowed. "What have you been up to?"

"Nothing," Celie said, still smiling. It was nothing but the truth. She had spent the night in a man's bed—in *Jace Tucker's* bed!—but she hadn't done a thing.

Yet.

Thinking about what she might do had her going hot and cold by turns. Just lying there watching Jace sleep, stroking his hair, holding him in her arms had made last night the most memorable of her life.

Which just, she thought with a certain amount of ironic self-awareness, went to show what a pitiful life she'd led so far.

Allison was still looking at her carefully, but Celie didn't say any more. She set to work shampooing her first customer, listening to the woman talk about how she was going to spend the day ashore on the private island that the cruise line leased.

It was billed as "the island idyll of your dreams," and it had everything—a beautiful pink sand beach for swimming, a reef for snorkeling, glass-bottom boats for those who weren't into getting wet, and Para-Sails, Jet Skis and Boogie Boards for those who were. There were volleyball and Frisbee for the sports aficionados, sand castle building contests for the artistically minded, a straw market for those who could never get enough of shopping, limbo dancing for the exhibitionists and, to top it off, a sort of Caribbean-island-barbecue-luau which pulled out all the gourmet stops.

It was a lot of fun. Celie had been there several times and she replied enthusiastically to the woman's questions and comments without even having to think about it. Instead she thought about Jace.

Was he still asleep? What would he think when he woke up? Would he even remember that she had been there? *She* would never forget.

The salon was reasonably busy. She and Allison had a

steady stream of people all morning. Marguerite, the receptionist, was on the phone taking appointments, and Simone, who disdained "island idylls" in favor of trips to the casinos of Paradise Island when they were in Nassau or night clubs in St. Maarten, was on hand, too, doing paperwork in the office and keeping an eye on things.

Once or twice Allison tried to get her to talk about where she'd been last night. But Celie wasn't doing that. She simply smiled and brushed the questions off—and drifted right back to thinking about Jace.

She hadn't wanted to leave him this morning. Nothing was settled. Nothing had been said. They hadn't talked. They'd only touched. Which was maybe just as well, she thought. She and Jace had never done very well with words.

It was still hard to imagine they were doing well at all. It was even hard to imagine a "they" that included just the two of them—as if they were a couple. How could they be a couple when they'd fought like cats and dogs or ignored each other for half her life?

What if she was completely wrong?

So she replayed it all again and again—from his fierce words last night to his kiss to his head in her lap as he slept only hours ago .

"I said a trim, my dear! A *trim!*" the woman in the chair said irritably and Celie jolted back to the present to discover she'd taken the woman's pageboy style to the bottom of her ear.

"Oh! Er, right. I…um…just wanted to even this out a little." Celie blushed, took a deep breath, and forced herself to concentrate on the business at hand. It wouldn't do to scalp the passengers just because she was shell-shocked. She could see Simone look at her through the glass that separated the salon from the office. She gave Celie a severe look.

Celie gave herself a little shake and studied the passenger's face. "Have you considered trying something a little shorter and layered? Like this?" She drew the woman's hair back, then fluffed it lightly out on the sides. It was less harsh. It softened her features, and the woman who had looked about to snap at her, blinked and reconsidered.

"Oh!" She turned her head to get another angle. Celie demonstrated what she had in mind. "Well," the woman said. "That might be interesting."

"It could be very flattering," Celie said. "It brings out your bone structure. Shall I?" She cocked her head and looked at the woman in the mirror.

The woman nodded. "Go ahead."

Celie smiled and began to snip, determined not to think about Jace for the moment. No sooner had she made the resolution than she almost took off the poor woman's ear when she looked up into the mirror to see Jace himself standing right behind her.

"Oh!" She jumped and snipped and—fortunately—did not draw blood. "I'm sorry," she babbled to the startled woman, but then she spun around, turning her attention wholly to Jace. "What are you doing here?"

Memories which had kept her entertained all morning—and which she had thought were vivid in the extreme—paled compared to the real man.

Jace stood, shaved and combed, lean and handsome, directly in front of her. He wore a pair of soft, faded Wranglers and a hunter-green polo shirt, and Celie had to admit that, as her dad used to say, he "cleaned up good."

Though his face was still a little pale, his color was coming back. His eyes were bright. He didn't look like death on the hoof any longer. On the contrary, he looked more drop-dead gorgeous than ever.

And judging from the look on her customer's face, she wasn't the only one to think so. The woman stared at him, openmouthed. So did the two ladies who were waiting. So did Allison. So did Marguerite. So did Simone.

Oh, dear.

"You said you were coming back." He looked at her intently.

"I was. But I got shanghaied into working. Stevie got sick."

"We need to talk." He didn't even seem to notice the attention he was attracting. He didn't seem to notice anything—or anyone—but her. And Celie barely saw anyone but him.

And then, out of the corner of her eye through the glass, she saw Simone get up out of her chair in the office. "We can't talk now," she said quickly, nodding toward the woman coming their way.

Jace didn't even glance at her. His eyes bored into Celie's. "Why not?"

"My boss," Celie began.

"Ah, the friend." Simone's voice cut in. She gave Jace a glacial smile and arched her perfect brows. "I thought we spoke before."

"We did." Jace brushed her off. "Now I need to talk to Celie."

"Celie is working. Do you wish an appointment, monsieur?"

"No, he just—" Celie began.

"Yes, I do," Jace said firmly. "I want an appointment with Celie."

Simone blinked. Her gaze narrowed momentarily, but when Jace stood his ground, she nodded and opened the schedule book and scanned the day. "Ah, too bad. I am afraid we are full," she said with evident satisfaction after a few moments' perusal. "No haircuts or massages from Mademoiselle O'Meara. What a pity." A saccharine smile appeared.

But Jace's attention was caught by something else. "Massages?" His brows lifted a mile.

"Therapeutic massage," Simone said flatly, "for neuro-muscular rehabilitation and relaxation. You understand?"

"Oh, yeah," Jace grinned. "I understand." But there was such obvious devilment in his tone that Celie was sure Simone knew she was being deliberately misunderstood. She winced as she considered how Simone would take that.

Simone evidently had no intention of taking it. She gave an audible sniff. "If you wish an appointment with Allison…" She nodded toward Celie's friend.

"No."

"Well, then, I am sorry. If you will excuse us…" Simone started to herd Jace toward the door the way Celie's dad had herded balky steers toward the corral.

Jace stiffened and remained unmoving. Anticipating disaster, Celie sucked in a quick breath. So did Allison. So did Marguerite. So did both the customers.

But after a long moment of collectively held breath, Jace shrugged. With one unreadable look at her, he nodded.

"Sure," he said, and turned on his heel to head for the door. When he got there, he stopped and looked back at Celie. "I'll be back."

She wondered if he would storm the salon. It didn't seem likely, but with Jace Tucker you never knew.

She worked until two cutting hair under Simone's unrelenting eagle eye. Then she moved to the relative peace of the spa where she took over Stevie's massage clients.

It was easier to think there with the soft Celtic music playing in the background and the scent of almond oil in the air. Easier, too, to dream of Jace.

Not to mention safer. No matter how much detail her mind indulged in as she replayed those hours she'd lain in bed with Jace, when she was giving a massage, Celie wasn't in danger of amputating anyone's ear.

It was therapeutic for her, too, in a way, she thought as she changed the sheets on the massage table in preparation for the last client of the day. She had spent the afternoon channeling all her longings into her work, into easing the stress and loosening the muscles in her clients.

One more and she would be finished. She buzzed Marguerite to send in her next appointment.

"Saving the best for last," she muttered when she looked at her list and saw who it was.

Gloria Campanella was what Armand had called "the first lady of the ship," a healthy, wealthy eighty-five-year-old widow who spent a good part of the year cruising from one port to another in search of heaven knew what.

"The cure for loneliness," Armand claimed. "The perfect mate."

Mrs. Campanella had been on three cruises since Celie had come aboard. She was always dressed to the nines, always had a martini in her hand, always had Stevie do her hair and give her a massage. He was her favorite, the only one who could soothe and charm her at the same time. Everyone else got the sharp side of her tongue. They all knew her—and knew not to cross her.

Then the door opened—and Jace walked in.

Celie stared. "What are you—?"

"I couldn't wait."

"But—Mrs. Campanella! You've got to get out of here! Mrs. Campanella will have a fit. She'll raise a stink. Simone will be furious!"

"Simone doesn't need to know."

But she would know. "Mrs. Campanella—"

"Mrs. Campanella changed her mind."

"What! She never!"

Jace nodded. "She did." He paused. "I bribed her."

"You never!" Celie was gaping at him.

But Jace nodded, perfectly serious. "She wasn't all that keen on getting a massage from you," he said cheerfully. "She prefers the guy."

"Yes, but—"

"I bought her a martini and listened to her life's story. She's a lonely old lady and she likes men. She especially—" he grinned "—likes cowboys."

Hard to imagine. But then, what he'd said was true. Mrs. Campanella did like men. Celie tried to envision tiny, immaculate Mrs. Campanella, who always reminded Celie of a well-dressed paperclip in her Felix Diamante designer originals, with Jace, in his jeans and shirt. It boggled the mind.

"She's not..." Celie waved a hand toward the waiting room, still expecting to hear Mrs. Campanella's strident tones demanding to know why she was being kept waiting.

"She's busy planning a trip to Elmer," Jace said. "I told her if she'd let me have her spot I'd get her a date with a ninety-year-old cowboy."

Celie's jaw dropped. "Artie?" *And Gloria Campanella?* Good God.

Jace grunted. "Figured it was the least he could do for the cause."

"What cause?"

"Us."

And there it was. There *they* were. Face-to-face at last.

Us. Celie O'Meara and Jace Tucker. Hardly stranger than Artie Gilliam and Gloria Campanella.

Their gazes met. Locked. Jace's eyes were bluer than the sea and even more unfathomable.

Celie wetted her lips nervously and cleared her throat. Us. He wasn't looking away.

"Did you..." she faltered, then tried again. "Did you really come on the cruise because...because of...me?"

In the background the Celtic tune wove its mysterious pattern. Outside Celie could hear the muffled calls of the exercise girl leading a group in calesthenics.

"Yeah," Jace said, his voice sounding as rusty as hers. "I did."

"But I thought—" She stopped and rethought, going over once more what she'd believed all these years. Then she shook her head. "I thought…you couldn't stand me," she told him.

Jace looked perplexed. "What? Why?"

"When Matt…when Matt brought you over that day, when he was going down the road with you…you barely even looked at me. You wanted nothing to do with me."

Jace looked away now. "Couldn't." He jammed his hands in his pockets and stared out the window at the sea.

"Couldn't?" Celie echoed. "Couldn't what?"

"Look at you! Want anything to do with you!"

She stared at him, mystified. "Why not?"

Jace rocked on his boot heels. A muscle ticked in his jaw. She thought for a long moment that he wasn't going to answer her. But then the words burst from him as he turned and glared at her. "Because, damn it, you were Matt's girl!"

"*What!*"

Jace hunched his shoulders, took a couple of steps away, but there was nowhere to go in the small room, so he turned and scowled straight at her. "You heard me."

She was Matt's girl.

"It mattered?" Celie asked, trying to work this out. It didn't fit with anything she had thought and was wholly new and surprising to her.

"A guy isn't supposed to want his buddy's girl." Jace growled.

Her mouth opened and closed silently as the implications

hit. He'd *wanted* her? All those years ago Jace Tucker had *wanted* her? The notion was absurd. And yet...

He was still glaring at her as if it were somehow her fault.

Finally she managed one tiny sound. "Oh."

Jace's mouth twisted. "Yeah. Oh." He raked a hand through his hair. "It seemed better not to have anything to do with you," he said.

She didn't know what to say. Her mind was whirling as she tried to put an entirely new interpretation on so many different events.

"You and Matt..." she began, trying to sort that out. "Did you..."

Jace ground his teeth. "I did not deliberately lead him astray." He bit out the words harshly. "Is that what you want to know?"

Numbly Celie nodded.

He shook his head. "I didn't," he swore. "Maybe I was a bad example—all right, I *was* a bad example. I did a lot of racketin' around in those days. But what he did, he did on his own."

"He wanted to be like you."

"The more fool he." Jace paced a couple more steps, did a little hop which, Celie suspected, had to do with nervous energy, then turned and confronted her again. "Look, I'm sorry it turned out the way it did—for you. You got hurt. He should've told you he wasn't ready. But really, Cel', you're better off without him."

"I know that," Celie said quietly.

Her agreement seemed to surprise him. "You do?"

She nodded. "In retrospect I could see he had been trying to tell me by leaving. Running off to the rodeo is not the sign of a man who wants to settle down." She smiled faintly. "I just didn't want to see it. I had my dreams."

The fault, she realized, had been at least half hers. She'd

been more in love with her dreams than she had been with Matt. He'd merely been the means to accomplishing them.

"It was just as well it happened," she said softly now.

"Yeah." Jace raked his fingers through his hair. "Well, you didn't exactly think so at the time." He took a deep breath. "You hated my guts."

"Yes."

"For a long time you hated my guts," he persisted.

Celie nodded. He was shaking his head, not understanding, and she knew she had to explain. "You knew I was a failure."

He stared at her. "Huh?"

"Matt dumped me!"

"Matt was an idiot. I thought we'd established that."

"No. He had his…oats…to sow," Celie said. "But I thought…I thought that—" her mouth seemed suddenly dry. She swallowed desperately. "Another woman might have been enough for him. Just…not me." She turned away, wouldn't look at Jace then. Couldn't believe she was having this conversation with him. She burned—her face, her neck, all of her.

"No," Jace sounded shocked. "Oh, no."

He took a step and reached out to catch her hand and draw her into his arms. Celie, for a moment, held back. But he persisted. He held her close, whispered her name against her lips. And then he kissed her.

This kiss was as deep and hungry and intense as the one he'd given her in his room two days ago. It spoke of longing and need and desire. And Celie was no proof against it. She stopped resisting and began to respond, to say with her kiss all the things she didn't think she would ever be able to put into words—things about pain and loss and anguish, about years of loneliness and emptiness, about hopes and dreams born anew.

It was Jace who finally broke it off, who stepped back,

shaken and flushed and breathing hard. "Whoa," he muttered, "unless you want to scandalize that dragon of a boss of yours."

Celie giggled. "She would be shocked!"

"Well, we wouldn't want to do that," Jace said with a lopsided grin. "Come on. Let's go finish this where we won't be disturbed."

"I can't."

He stared at her. "What? Why the hell not?"

"I can't leave. Not now. Not until six. She'll be checking."

Jace looked poleaxed. "Who cares?"

"It's my job!"

He started to say something, then closed his mouth again and nodded. "Okay. Fine. Let's get on with it then."

Celie blinked. "Get on with what?"

The lopsided grin was back. "My massage."

"You want a massage?" Celie said with a smile after looking momentarily startled.

"Unless you're chicken?" Jace teased recklessly.

She smiled. "We'll see who's chicken."

Jace had a feeling it was going to be him.

"Strip down to your shorts," Celie said briskly. "I'll give you a few minutes."

"You don't have to leave—" he began to protest, but she was already out the door.

Grinning, anticipating, he stripped down to his shorts, then boosted himself up onto the massage table, relishing the thought of her hands on him for an hour.

When she came back, she turned on a CD of some sort of soft lilting Celtic tune that reminded him of a movie he'd seen.

Jace's mouth quirked into a grin. "Music to sink a ship by?"

Celie ignored him. "Lie on your stomach and put your face in the face cradle. Let your arms go loose."

Jace did as she instructed, settling on the sheet she had warmed with a heating pad. She folded another sheet over him, baring only his back and shoulders. He heard her rub her hands together and felt his anticipation grow. That wasn't the only thing that was growing.

Cool it, buddy, he advised himself. If he was going to last the hour, he was going to have to think pure thoughts and multiplication tables. Indeed the first touch of her hands sent a jolt right through him. She'd only touched his back, between his shoulders, but his mind sent impulses zinging from his back to his brain to his groin like lightning strikes.

Celie paused, her hands resting lightly on his back. "You're very tense."

"I'm very horny," Jace corrected.

"We'll take care of that," she promised.

That startled him. "Here?" he said, aghast.

"Oh, yes," Celie said, stunning him.

But it wasn't long before he realized that she didn't mean what he thought she'd meant.

He'd expected to lie there and allow Celie to work her magic on him, seducing him with her hands. Instead she found every injury he'd ever had and ferreted out every single protesting muscle and bit of scar tissue.

He was lulled at first by the strong smooth strokes on his back and shoulders, and he gave himself up to it until her fingers slowed and she traced old scars and sore spots and probed lightly.

"Does this hurt?"

"No," he lied, wanting her to move on.

But she kneaded some more, deepening the massage. "How about this?"

"What are you, a sadist?"

"No. But it's tight. I can feel it knotted up there. Let me

see if we can't work it out. I do a terrific neuro-muscular massage.''

So much for seduction.

''It will feel better when I'm done,'' she promised.

''Like it feels so much better to stop banging your head against the wall?''

Celie laughed. ''You could say that.''

She worked over each and every tender spot he'd ever had in his life—in his neck, on his back, on the shoulder of his riding arm. She found the spots where he'd broken ribs, the vertebrae he'd cracked in his back. With her thumbs and fingers she rubbed them gently, then more deeply, and finally began digging her fingers down to lift and roll the muscle.

''Jeez!'' The word whistled through Jace's teeth, arousal fading fast.

''Too much?'' Celie asked, her voice concerned. ''If it is, say so. I tend to get a little carried away trying to work out these spasms.''

''It's okay,'' Jace said gruffly.

Her thumbs kneaded the cords of his neck, pressing up into his scalp, sending goose bumps down across his shoulders and back. Then she worked over his neck and shoulders and down his back, her fingers and thumbs walking up and down his spine, stopping to find the bunched muscles, kneading them, working the spasms out.

It wasn't seductive—not the way Jace had imagined it. But like the time they'd spent together in bed last night, it felt good. It felt…right.

She moved on to his legs.

''Ah,'' she said softly as he tensed when she touched the one he'd broken at the finals last December. ''That still hurts, does it?''

''It's…a little tender.''

''I'll take care of it.''

She did his other leg first, rubbing and kneading, warming it and stretching it, before she left it tingling and moved on to the one he had broken.

She bent his knee, testing his range of motion first. Then starting from his heel, she began working her way up the muscles in his calf. At first it hurt a lot. His leg always hurt a lot. He'd got used to it, had tried to learn to live with it. Had never really considered that it wouldn't. But now, as Celie worked on him, gradually the hard tight spots seemed to soften and relax.

"Ah." He couldn't help the sound escaping. He leg felt so much better, looser, less tense.

"Better?" Celie asked.

He nodded. "Yeah. Oh, yeah."

"Good." She moved up above his knee and began working on the hamstring, easing the tension there, as well. And it worked.

"Great," he murmured. "Thanks."

"Still horny?" she asked lightly.

Jace grimaced, realizing he was not. "I could be again in a few minutes," he said hopefully.

Silently Celie ran her hands up the backs of his legs. Her fingers felt very different all of a sudden. Intimate. Personal. Very personal.

Jace's body went on alert as the fingers moved up over his butt and traced the waistband of his shorts. It didn't take him a few minutes to get horny again. A few seconds, more like.

He turned his head to look back over his shoulder at her. "Celie?"

She gave him a smile, then consulted her watch. "Oh, gee," she said with a grin now wholly unrepentant. Her eyes danced. "Time's up."

Seven

It wasn't the devil who made her do it, but there was definitely an impish rogue hidden somewhere inside Celie's head who dared her to dare Jace.

Because that's what it was—those fingers, there at the end of a perfectly legitimate massage, dancing up the back of his thighs—a dare. They'd gone from skilled professionalism to tempting teasing in seconds. They wanted what Celie had wanted all along.

She'd wanted it at the very beginning. She could have turned the massage into a seduction at any point. She hadn't because she was at work. She had standards to uphold, and she intended to uphold them.

Even with Jace.

Besides, it had been quickly apparent that Jace needed something she had it in her power to give. He was a rodeo cowboy. Rodeo cowboys, by definition, hurt. It was the name of the game. And old rodeo cowboys went on hurting even after they'd given up the game.

They were walking masses of scar tissue, muscle spasms and various and sundry contusions and adhesions. Jace was no exception.

Last night in bed she'd seen old scars. She'd touched them lightly as he slept. She'd wondered how he'd got each one and thought someday, perhaps, he'd tell her.

In the meantime, though, today for an hour, she'd done her best to ease those pains.

If Simone had got wind of his deal with Mrs. Campanella and come to see exactly what was going on, she'd have seen exactly what she was supposed to see—Celie acting like what she was: a professional massage therapist.

Until the last few seconds, when she'd turned into the woman who wanted to make love with Jace.

"You," he told her, rolling over so fast she thought he might flip right off the table, "are asking for it, Celie O'Meara."

She fluttered her eyelashes at him. "I am?"

He leaped off the table like a man who had no aches and pains at all, grabbing her around the waist and hauling her into his arms. It took no imagination at all to figure out how aroused he was.

"Jace!"

"Don't start something you don't intend to finish," he muttered against her lips.

"I intend to finish it," Celie said. "I *want* to finish it. But not here."

"Then let's get out of here. I presume you're finished now? Do you have to sign out with the dragon?"

Celie shook her head. "No. I just have a few things to take care of. Quick things," she promised when he glared at her.

"Damn quick," Jace insisted.

"Yes. You get dressed. I'll finish up." She stripped the

bed linens off the massage table and started toward the door.

Jace caught her by the hand and tugged her around. "You're not going to disappear."

Celie smiled. "I'm not going to disappear."

He felt like a teenager. Gauche and awkward. Eager, yet desperate.

For a guy who'd relished—and deserved—his reputation as a ladies' man, Jace felt like a dumb kid now.

He'd practically dragged her to his stateroom. But the minute he got her there and shut the door, everything changed. He leaned against the door, his palms sweating, his breathing shallow. And not from arousal. From nerves.

He was going to make love with Celie O'Meara.

And his stomach was clenching and his body was quivering, and if he didn't get his act together, he was going to make a complete mess of it. If it hadn't mattered so much, he'd have laughed at himself.

Jace Tucker, panic-stricken at the thought of taking a woman to bed?

No, not *a* woman. She wasn't just any woman.

She was the only woman who'd really ever mattered—and that made all the difference.

Every other time Jace had gone to bed with a woman, it had been to have a good time then and there. He'd always been a generous bed partner, always happy to make sure his companion enjoyed it as much as he did. But the act itself had never had a deeper meaning, had never gone beyond the physical. It had been fun. It had provided a release. And always he'd been able to walk away without looking back.

No more.

He couldn't walk away from Celie. And it wasn't just *his* body, *his* mind, *his* heart and *his* soul that were in-

volved. It was *Celie's,* too. He had to make it right for her.
Had to make it beautiful for her. Had to show her how
much he loved her.

For a guy who wrote the book on lack of commitment,
this was pretty scary stuff. In fact, it was damn near para-
lyzing.

"Is something wrong?" Celie asked. She was looking at
him curiously as she stood by his bed, apparently without
a qualm in the world, already unbuttoning her shirt. She
smiled and peeled it off her shoulders, baring a tanned mid-
riff and full breasts covered by the peach-colored lace of
her bra. Her hands went to unfasten the front-clasped bra.

Cripes, she was going to be naked before he got his boots
unnailed from the floor. "Stop!"

At his exclamation, Celie stopped. She stared, her fingers
stilled on the clasp of her bra. "What?"

"I want…" He swallowed. His mouth felt like the Sa-
hara. He cleared his throat desperately and tried again. "I
want to do that."

Celie's hands dropped to her sides. She nodded—and
stood waiting for him.

He almost tripped over his boots, crossing the few feet
of carpet between them, until he was standing right in front
of her, looking down on the rise and fall of her breasts
beneath the lace. He took a breath and put his fingers to
work on the clasp. They were like thumbs—a tenth-grader's
thumbs! He was mortified watching them tremble.

He flicked his eyelids up to see if she was laughing at
him. He wouldn't have been surprised. But she wasn't
laughing at all. Her lower lip was caught in her teeth and
she was trembling, too.

It made him feel better. He got her bra undone. Opened
it. Feasted his gaze on full, creamy breasts. He smiled.
"Ah."

He caressed them with his thumbs and fingers, his palms

brushing her nipples. He saw her suck in her breath and felt her shudder. She didn't move, though, just clenched her fists at her sides and remained absolutely still as his hands stroked her. Beneath his fingers he could feel her shallow, unsteady breathing. He could hear the faint gasp of her breath as he explored her further, letting his hands mould the shape of her rib cage, then settle at her waist, then slide a finger inside the waistband of her jeans.

Her stomach muscles clenched. "Jace!"

"Mmm?" He bent his head, dropped kisses along one shoulder, then across her jaw and neck and across the other shoulder. With his tongue he touched her heated flesh. He nipped and tasted, and she shuddered, and suddenly her arms wrapped hard around his waist.

She pulled his shirt out of his jeans and slid her hands up underneath it to caress his back. There was nothing professional about her touch now. Her caresses were as heated and hungry as his. She grasped the hem of his shirt and drew it up and over his head, then tossed it aside and pressed her palms against his chest.

Her thumbs rubbed over his nipples and were immediately followed by her tongue. Jace sucked air. His fingers tightened on her buttocks and pulled her hard against him, letting her feel his urgency. "Careful," he muttered.

But Celie shook her head and continued the hot wet kisses. "I've been careful way too long already." And her fingers began to work on the buckle of his belt.

Telling him she'd had enough of being careful was like throwing kerosene on a roaring fire. It did no good to bank the flames now. There was no chance to slow things down, to throw a little water on their passion. All Jace's worries were overtaken by desire. All of his panic was swallowed by need.

He'd waited forever. At least it seemed that way. "You're sure?" he rasped.

But she'd got his belt undone by then, and when her fingers slid down the zipper of his jeans, Jace had all the answer he needed.

As she freed him and he felt the cool air hit his heated, hungry flesh, he was tearing at Celie's jeans, making quick work of them, unfastening, unzipping, peeling them and her panties, in one deft movement, over her hips and down her legs.

She kicked them aside and pushed his down as well. They tangled around his boots and he stumbled and muttered a curse as they tumbled together onto the bed.

"Sorry," he mumbled, then swallowed the word in a gasp as her fingers traced the burning length of him.

"I'm not." Celie wriggled beneath him, making him crazy, bringing him to the verge of forgetting every sane, sensible thought he'd had about going slow and taking time and making it perfect for her.

"Cel'! Wait! Slow down! I—"

"Can't keep up?" she whispered against his lips, smiling at him while her hands drove him to distraction.

He grabbed them and held them, pinned her to the bed with the weight of him and took a shuddering breath as he looked down into her eyes. "I want," he said with difficulty, "for it to be good for you. I want it to be perfect for you. I don't want to…to take—" He stumbled over this last as she moved beneath him and the feel of her made him catch his breath. "I want it to be right."

Celie lifted her head to bring her lips to his. She kissed him softly, lingeringly. "It *is* right, Jace." She kissed him again, traced his lips with her tongue, raised her hips against his, rocking them together. "Take me."

He did.

He couldn't wait any longer. He'd waited forever. He needed her now.

And from the way she clutched at him, opened for him

and drew him in, Celie seemed to need him, too. Her fingers dug into his back, her head tossed, and once more her hips lifted to welcome his thrust. "Come to me, Jace."

"Yesss." The word whistled through his teeth. He had Celie beneath him, Celie surrounding him, Celie loving him. At last.

At last, Celie thought.

It was the stuff of dreams. Of fantasies. Of thousands of nights of loneliness finally filled. It was Jace Tucker doing the most wonderful things to her, stroking her, touching her, kissing her, wanting it to be right for her.

It *was* right for her. It was the most right thing she'd ever done—welcoming him into her body as well as into her heart. Loving Jace was finding the other half of her soul.

And when he filled her, stroked her, shattered her—and himself—he took the pieces of all her broken dreams and once again made them whole.

He lay, spent, still shuddering on top of her, knowing he should move, that his weight had to be too much for her. And yet when he tried to, she held him fast.

"No," she whispered, hands clasped against the small of his back.

He lifted his head to look down at her, and the sight that met his eyes stabbed him to the core. "Oh, God. Did I hurt you?"

He'd never made a woman cry before!

But Celie shook her head and smiled through her tears. "You didn't hurt me at all. It was wonderful. Marvelous. *You're* wonderful. Marvelous."

Jace blinked. He was? "Then why—"

She shook her head again and swiped at her eyes. "I always cry when I'm happy."

She was happy. She was in his arms, and she was happy.

Jace grinned, happy, too. Happier than he'd ever been in his life.

He laughed out loud and rolled over, hauling her on top of him. Her legs tangled with his, caught in the jeans and boots he'd never managed to shed. She sat up and began to extricate herself—and stripped off his boots and jeans, as well.

She ran her hands over him. Intimately. Possessively.

His breathing quickened. His own desire was immediately rekindled. And he reached for her, drew her back into his arms and began to love her again. Slowly this time. Tenderly. With all the finesse he'd lacked before. And she watched him, touched him, smiled at him.

The phone rang.

Jace jerked, biting off a curse as he reached over and grabbed it. "What?" he barked.

"Just wonderin' if you been makin' any progress," Artie said cheerfully.

"Yes," Jace said. "Go away."

As a girl Celie had imagined more romantic interludes than she could remember. She'd dreamed of mountain idylls, walks on a moonlit beach, dinners for two on a cozy terrace, and a hundred other incredible settings where she and the man of her dreams would commit themselves to each other forever.

But even Celie didn't believe it would happen just that way.

The next day they sailed all day—and Celie, of course, worked while Jace stayed out of Simone's way.

"I don't even want her to see you," Celie said. "I don't want her to think anything happened."

Jace just grinned. "She's only got to look at you to know something happened," he said with considerable satisfaction.

Celie felt herself turn red, and one look in the mirror in Jace's stateroom told her he was speaking the truth. Her eyes were sparkling, her mouth looked well kissed, and she actually seemed to glow.

It was embarrassing. It was wonderful.

"I don't want you coming there," she said severely.

Jace's grin grew even more wicked. "I don't want to come there, either," he said, deadpan. He wrapped her in his arms and pulled her hard against him, so that even after a night of loving she could feel his growing arousal. "I want to come here. With you."

"Stop that! Behave." She pulled back and shook her finger at him.

He caught it and nibbled the end of it, sending a shaft of longing streaking through her, too. "You don't want me to behave," he said gruffly, and his eyes dared her to deny him.

"What I want has nothing to do with it," Celie said firmly. "I work here. I have to do my job."

"Tomorrow you're off, though? When we get to St. Maarten?"

"Unless Stevie is still sick," Celie agreed, "and I have to cover for him again, yes. I should be able to go ashore."

"Stevie won't be sick."

"You know that, do you?"

"He won't dare."

And he didn't. He was there bright and early when Celie went to check in. She half expected Simone, who obviously knew something was going on, to come up with some other way of preventing her from spending the day with Jace. But Simone was busy when Celie breezed in, and she didn't even look up.

"Have fun," Stevie called after her, grinning.

"I will," Celie said as she hurried to join Jace to go ashore.

It was the day she'd always dreamed of. The streets of Philipsburg, the port city on the Dutch side of St. Maarten, were crowded with tourists from ships as well as with other vacationers. It was hot and, away from the beach, there was little breeze.

But it didn't matter. They were together, hand in hand, hips and shoulders brushing as they prowled the narrow streets. Jace bought her a straw hat to keep the sun off, and Celie insisted that she get him a pair of shorts and a pair sandals so he wouldn't have to spend the day in jeans and boots.

"Nothin' wrong with jeans and boots," Jace protested when she dragged him into one of the *steegjes,* the little lanes between Front Street and Back Street where she found a casual-clothing store.

"Nothing at all," she said. "Jeans and boots are fine for Montana. Not for here. You'll be too hot. Besides," she grinned, when he came back out of the dressing room wearing a pair of shorts and looking self-conscious, "I like looking at your legs."

A flush crept up Jace's neck. "Celie! You're not supposed to say things like that," he growled, clearly embarrassed, as the clerk smiled.

Celie, unrepentant, just laughed. It was true—she did like looking at his legs. And, freed from constraints at last, she was going to enjoy every minute of it. For years she had tried not to look at him at all. Now she couldn't seem to stop.

She'd awakened early this morning and had resisted going back to sleep even though they'd been awake most of the night. Instead she'd simply lain there and feasted her eyes on Jace. She had traced the hard good looks, tough sinewy muscles, and the myriad nicks and scars on his taut, tanned skin that made him Jace. He was beautiful, she'd thought.

Though she knew if she ever told him that, he'd blush even more deeply than he was right now as the clerk handed him a carrier bag with his jeans and boots. He stood staring in dismay down at his bare, hair-roughened legs.

"I feel naked," he complained.

"Not even close," Celie said. "But if you want to really feel naked, we could go to the beach."

"A nude beach?" Jace said mockingly.

"If you want."

He gave her a hard look, decided she was joking and said, "Right. Let's go."

She took him by the hand and said, "Follow me."

Armand had been only too happy to see to her "education" the first time she'd come to St. Maarten. He'd blithely suggested they go to the beach, and she had agreed, only discovering after they arrived that clothing was optional. To his dismay she'd opted for it, insisting on wearing her bathing suit, as she had the two subsequent times she'd come.

She didn't know what she would do if Jace willingly doffed his clothes. But she didn't need to worry. He took one look, his jaw dropped, and he began hauling her in the other direction.

"No way," he said. "No blinkin' way!"

Celie grinned at him. "You don't want to strip off?"

"Me?" He shrugged as if that hadn't even occurred to him. "Hell, nobody's gonna look at me. I don't want a bunch of guys gawking at you!"

They went to another beach a distance away where they both wore bathing suits, and Celie got to put lotion on Jace and he got to put lotion on her, and afterward he muttered thickly that maybe they should just forget the beach and get a launch back to the ship.

But Celie said no. "You'll love the water. Come on!" And she jumped up and took off running toward the water.

Cursing, Jace levered himself up and chased her into the surf. And he did love it. They swam and played in the clear blue water and then lay side by side on the beach to dry off before heading off to have lunch.

There was no shortage of options for the meal—everything from gourmet French restaurants in Grand Case to you'd-think-you-were-in-the-states hamburger joints. They opted for conch fritters and cold beer at a sidewalk café where they could sit and watch the people passing by.

Except, Celie realized, they only seemed to have eyes for each other. Jace fed her a conch fritter dipped in saffron sauce, and she nibbled it all the way down till she was nibbling his thumb.

"You don't maybe want to go back to the ship?" he said plaintively.

But Celie just grinned and shook her head. "Not yet." The day was too perfect, too beautiful. She would savor it for a lifetime.

After they'd eaten, they walked around some more, looking in shops. There were a thousand of them, selling everything from diamonds and Rolex watches to seashells and silly T-shirts. Celie wanted to find presents for her mother and Walt, for Sara's soon-to-be-born baby and for Artie.

"I owe him," she said. "We both do. We need to find the perfect gift."

Jace groaned. "You look. I'll have another beer." He nodded hopefully toward a bar across the street where reggae music was pouring out. There were some lengths, Celie realized, to which even fairy-tale days didn't extend. Expecting Jace to enjoy shopping was one of them.

"All right. I'll meet you at the bar in an hour."

"Sure." He headed across the street eagerly. Celie, watching him go, thought he looked almost as good in shorts as he did in Wranglers.

He looked best of all, though, in absolutely nothing. Her

cheeks warmed at the thought—and at the memory of his lean, hard, bare body. She giggled, amazed at how free and comfortable she felt thinking that way about him. It was as if all the desire and need and dreams that she'd held pent-up inside for years had suddenly found their focus and come pouring out. Which was pretty much the truth.

She was half tempted to run after him and agree to go back to the ship right now. But she did want to get something for Artie.

They really did owe Artie. A lot.

She got her mother and Walt a photo album for the pictures of their own travels. They had gone to Vietnam this summer to meet Walt's daughter. She was sure there would be plenty of photos to fill the album. She got Sara's baby a romper set with pineapples and palm trees on it and a CD of nursery songs set in reggae style.

Artie was harder to buy for.

What did you get a ninety-year-old man who might not have everything, but who certainly had virtually everything he needed or might want?

What he would want, Celie decided, was to share a part of the cruise. So she ended up buying him a photo album, too. Then she got a couple of disposable cameras so she could take pictures of all the places she and Jace went. That way he could see where they had been. It had, after all, been his determination that had finally got them together. They might have gone on forever at cross purposes if he hadn't insisted on Jace coming on the cruise.

She'd walked halfway down Front Street before she found everything she wanted. But finally, clutching her purchases, she hurried back to the bar. Jace was there, drinking a beer with the three blondes from the ship.

Seeing him surrounded by women, Celie felt momentarily awkward. But as soon as he saw her, a grin lit his face.

"Ah, good. Gotta go," he said to the blondes. He left them and his beer to join her.

"You didn't have to leave," Celie said quickly.

But he took her hand and walked her back out into the street. "Yes, I did. Where do you want to go now?"

It was getting on toward evening. They would have to be back at the launch in an hour or so. "How about just walking on the cliffs overlooking the beach?" Celie suggested.

Armand had shown her the cliffs above Cupecoy Beach. In her most recent romantic dreams, she'd imagined meeting her perfect man and walking there hand in hand with him.

Jace smiled. "Sounds good."

Celie took a picture of Jace in front of the bar, and then he took one of her. And then they got a passerby to take one of them together. "For Artie," she said. "We're taking pictures for him to share our trip."

"Of some things," Jace agreed. "Not everything."

Celie smiled. "No, not everything."

But on their way to the cliffs they stopped and took photos of the other places they'd been in St. Maarten. Then they took a taxi up to the cliffs. "Half an hour," Jace told the driver.

It was every bit as beautiful as she'd dreamed it would be, with the sun going down and the sky turning pink and orange and purple. The breeze ruffled her hair and touched her sunburned cheeks, and she turned and smiled at Jace.

"Isn't it beautiful?" she said.

"Mmm," he murmured. But he wasn't looking at the view at all. He was looking at her. He had hold of one of her hands and he drew her close and lifted his other hand to cup the back of her neck and tilt her face up to meet his.

And then he kissed her.

He tasted of the sea and the sun and the spicy saffron dip from the conch fritters. His mouth was hard and warm and persuasive against hers, and Celie responded, fulfilling her dream, kissing him in return, loving him, wanting this moment to go on forever.

And then Jace broke off the kiss and stepped back.

Bereft, Celie opened her eyes to see what was wrong. "Jace?"

His face was inches from hers, his eyes dark and intent. "I love you," he said, his voice ragged. "Marry me."

And Celie knew only one answer to that.

"Yes," she whispered, and wrapped her arms around him to kiss him again. "Oh, yes."

Eight

"It is a shipboard romance," Simone said firmly, fixing Celie with a hard stare. "Zat is all."

"It's *not* all," Celie protested. "Besides, I didn't meet him on the ship. I've known him for years."

"Humph." Simone shook her head disapprovingly. "Even so. Everyone knows ze shipboard romances, zey don't last."

"Ours will," Celie insisted. "We're getting married! We've set the date." Celie waved her left hand in front of Simone's doubting gaze. On her ring finger was the solitaire diamond ring that Jace had given her last night when he'd asked her to marry him.

She'd been astonished to see the tiny black-velvet-covered box he'd pulled out of his pocket. "Wherever did you—" She'd stared at it, and then at him, amazed.

Jace had simply grinned. "You weren't the only one who went shopping."

While she had been out buying photo albums and cameras and rompers with pineapples on them for her family and Artie, it seemed that Jace had been buying her a diamond!

"He said I could bring it back," he'd told her almost diffidently, "if you don't like it. Or if—" he grimaced "—if you'd said no."

"I love it," Celie had said. And she certainly hadn't said no. It was the stuff of dreams. She might not even believe it now if she couldn't look at the ring on her finger. It was a simple, elegant solitaire with a white-gold band. Very traditional. Absolutely perfect.

Simone looked at it and sighed mightily. "Shipboard romance! It doesn't last," she repeated. "And if you quit before your six-monz commitment is over, Celie, you will not be able to come back."

"I don't want to come back," Celie said stubbornly. "I never wanted to do this forever. I only wanted to travel, to see the world, to meet people—"

"To meet a man," Simone said.

Celie flushed. "Well, yes," she admitted. "But I certainly never thought it would be Jace."

But it was Jace—and she had the ring and the man to prove it. "We're getting married on October third," she told Simone.

Jace had suggested they get married right away. "We can get married on the ship," he'd argued. "People do."

But Celie had shaken her head. "I don't want to get married on the ship. I want to get married at home. In Elmer." It would make up for the last time, for Matt's defection, for having to call everything off.

Jace hadn't been thrilled. "Are you sure?"

"Yes." Celie had been adamant. "I want to get married at home."

She was just as adamant now with Simone. "I'm going

home. I'm handing in my notice. I don't care if I can't come back. I don't *want* to come back!''

"Zey all say zat." Simone sighed wearily. "And zen, two months later…" She gave a mournful shake of her head.

Celie ignored her. Undoubtedly Simone had dealt with plenty of starry-eyed young women over the years, women who'd thought they'd met the man of their dreams—only to discover they were wrong, that the men were nightmares.

But she was not one of those women.

And Jace was not one of those men.

It wasn't the same. It wasn't the same at all.

"You are going home? Getting married?" Armand's eyebrows lifted in surprise at the sight of the ring on Celie's finger.

She had spotted him in the staff lounge and had gone over to say goodbye and, maybe if she was honest, to prove that there was another man in the world who didn't think she was naive and basically hopeless.

"Tomorrow's my last day," she told him.

"So soon you quit? Must be very persuasive." He waggled dark eyebrows. "And who is the lucky man?"

"A man I knew at home."

"Ah, yes. Of course." Armand nodded understandingly

"What do you mean, of course?" Celie demanded.

Armand gave a negligent shrug. "Just that he is, how do you say…? A homebody, too."

"He's hardly a homebody." It was hard to imagine anyone describing Jace that way. As long as she'd known him he'd always been a moving-on, show-me-the-bright-lights sort of guy. But Armand didn't know that.

"Is better for you to be there," he approved. "Is where you belong…in the home with children and puppies, yes?"

He looked her up and down critically, then nodded in satisfaction. "I always think you look like a wife."

Coming from Armand, that was not necessarily a compliment. But Celie couldn't really argue with him. Nor did she want to. After all, a wife was exactly what she had always wanted to be.

She smiled. "Thank you. I just came to say goodbye," she told him. "And, thank you for the...um, education, too." She smiled a little wryly. "It was...interesting."

Armand grinned and winked at her. Then he kissed her lightly on both cheeks. "Always I am happy to educate. Be happy, *ma petite.*"

Artie and her mother were at the airport to meet them.

"Is it true?" Joyce demanded, hurrying toward them, eager eyes going from Celie to Jace and back again. "Artie says you're getting married?" She sounded as if she didn't trust Artie not to be pulling her leg.

But Celie, beaming, held out her hand for her mother to inspect the ring, and Joyce gave a little cry of delight. "Oh, darling, how wonderful." She wrapped Celie in a fierce hug, then reached out and dragged Jace into a three-way embrace.

Then she gave him a smacking kiss. "You dark horse, you," she chided him. "I had no idea."

Artie huffed. "Tol' her, didn't I? An' they say women are the romantics." He shook his head in dismay. Then he winked at Jace. "Told ya so."

Jace grinned, looking both embarrassed and pleased. But then he protested, "I coulda done it myself."

"Yeah, right." Artie snorted. "In which century? Hell's bells, boy, I ain't gonna live forever, an' the rate you two were goin', I'd'a had to. If I wanted to see the two of you hitched, I reckoned it was up to me to kick you in the tail and get you movin'."

"Right," Jace said dryly. "It was all your idea."

"Mebbe not all," Artie allowed as they moved toward the baggage claim. "I can't say I would a picked out such a purty engagement ring." He put an arm around Celie's shoulder and gave her a squeeze. "Sure am glad you're home, missy."

Celie looped an arm around his narrow waist. "Me, too."

"I've got a stew simmering." Joyce herded them down the stairs. "You'll all come and eat with us, of course. And you can stay with us, if you want," she said to her daughter.

In their new home, Joyce meant. The one Walt had just finished building on his ranch. Last year he'd turned the old house over to his daughter, Cait, and her new husband, Charlie.

"Thanks, but I think I'll stay in town," Celie said. "At the house—if you don't think Polly will mind." The huge, rambling two-story Victorian just off the main street of Elmer where they had all lived until this spring still belonged to Polly, after all, even though she and the kids had moved to Sloan's ranch as soon as school was out.

"I'm sure Polly won't care at all," Joyce said. "She'll probably be glad to have someone in there instead of leaving it empty. Now that she and the kids are up at Sloan's place, I think she's planning to sell it."

"She is?" Celie didn't like the thought of that. There were so many memories associated with that house. "Maybe we could buy it," she said to Jace. "It would be close to the store if you're going to stay at Artie's. And I could reopen The Spa," she added eagerly.

"I was thinkin' of building a place out by Ray and Jodie," Jace said as he grabbed their bags off the luggage carousel and led the way toward the parking area. "I'm gonna be training horses out there."

"Whichever," Celie said happily. "We can discuss it later. We have other things to think about now." She grinned. "Like the wedding."

"About the wedding…" Joyce looked at her daughter a little worriedly, and Celie knew she was remembering the last wedding.

"Thought mebbe you'd a got married on the ship," Artie said.

"No." Celie shook her head. "I wanted to get married here. This time it will be perfect," she said, looping her arm through Jace's and smiling up at him.

"Yep," he said equably. He glanced back at her mother and Artie. "Told her I'd get married anytime, anywhere."

"But we had to come back here. We couldn't get married without Artie," Celie said. "Or the family."

"I could have." Jace tossed the bags in the back of Walt's crew-cab truck that Joyce had driven over. "Don't matter to me."

"Well, it matters to me," Celie said.

She had been dreaming about this wedding for years.

Artie was stretched out in his easy chair, his feet stuck up on the hassock, as he regarded Jace over the top of a glass of Jack Daniel's. In his lap was the photo album Celie had given him. He had studied it with considerable satisfaction, nodding and smiling while Celie had been there. But now she was gone and he was looking at it again and still nodding.

"See, what'd I tell you?" He said to Jace. "Worked like a charm."

"Not exactly a charm," Jace countered mildly. He wasn't telling Artie about all the bad times. It was enough to remember them himself. He settled into the sofa, balancing his own glass of Jack Daniel's on his belt buckle. The Jack Daniel's had been his gift to Artie.

He figured they'd need a damn sight more of it before this wedding was done. After two weeks at home, he'd barely had a chance to sit down and take a deep breath. He worked, of course, for Artie and on the ranch, and he trained horses every morning for Taggart Jones. But every second he wasn't working, his presence had been demanded by Celie, and he'd been presented with a thousand options for wedding plans.

"Why the heck should I care whether we have a sit-down dinner or a stand-up buffet?" he groused. "And what difference does it make what kind of paper the invitations are on? Why can't we just call people up and invite 'em to come?"

Artie sipped the Jack Daniel's and gave an appreciative sigh. "She's gonna marry you, ain't she? Well, then, quitcher fussin'. Everything's hunky-dory."

"And I gotta wear a tux," Jace went on, aggrieved.

Clothing had already been discussed. It wasn't, to Jace's dismay, "optional." Celie was going to do things right and proper, and that, she told him, meant a floor-length gown for her and her bridesmaids and tuxes for him and his best man.

Artie was going to be the best man.

That was the only thing Jace had insisted on when Celie had gone into wedding-planning mode. He owed the old man—and he couldn't think of a better way of paying him back. The fact that Artie would have to wear a tux, too, made it a little bit sweeter.

Jace had wondered if Celie would argue that having a ninety-year-old best man would upset her "perfect" wedding pictures. But she hadn't argued at all. In fact, she'd been delighted at the idea.

She'd only frowned for a moment as she'd wondered: if Artie was the best man, who was going to give her away.

"Walt," Jace had suggested. He was, after all, Celie's mother's husband.

"He could," Celie agreed. "Or Jack." Her ten-year-old nephew. Then she'd brightened. "I know! I'll get Sloan to do it!"

"Don't you dare! He'll turn our wedding into some media circus!" He remembered all too well what a colossal to-do Sloan's presence had made of the Great Montana Cowboy Auction.

"No media circus," Celie had promised. "Very low-key. We won't tell anyone."

"This is Elmer. Everyone will know."

"But everyone knows Sloan, too, so it won't be a big deal. And we'll keep the media out."

"We're definitely keeping the media out." There was no question about that. Not, Jace was sure, that the media would even care that he was marrying Celie O'Meara.

The only person who cared was him. He cared desperately. He loved her desperately. He wanted her to be happy. That was the only reason he was putting up with all of this.

The past two weeks had been insane. Celie had been glued to her wedding planner. She'd been talking nonstop to her mother, to Poppy Nichols, who ran a florist shop down in Livingston, to Milly Callahan, whose dad, John, was a grocer who knew a caterer, to the caterer, to the stationer, to the minister at the local church, to Polly to arrange for renting the town hall.

Jace had wanted to celebrate their engagement by going home, locking the doors and taking Celie to bed.

"We can't do that," Celie had said, horrified.

"We can't? Why not?"

"Because this is Elmer! Everyone will know!"

"They know, anyway," Jace had argued.

But Celie had been firm. She wasn't having Alice Benn or Cloris Stedman or any of the other moral citizens of

Elmer scandalized by their behavior. "What would Artie think?" she'd demanded.

"Artie," Jace had said with absolute conviction, "will be all for it."

Now Artie stretched, sipped his Jack Daniel's and said, "Dunno what yer doin' here. How come you ain't over at Celie's?"

"Because," Jace said, "that is Command Central, and if I go over there she will give me a list of things to do."

"Beginnin' as she means to go on, is she?" Artie chuckled.

"I damned well hope not," Jace said. "I hope she comes to her senses. Soon."

He reckoned he could have put together half a dozen perfectly legal weddings and had time left over to brand a herd of cattle in the past two weeks.

"This thing is turnin' into the wedding that ate Montana," he grumbled now, shuddering again at the thought of tuxedos. "What's wrong with boots and jeans?"

"Beats me." Artie yawned. "Shoulda married her 'fore you left the ship."

"I suggested it. She said no."

"Should've grabbed her by the hair and yanked her right up b'fore the captain."

"Now you tell me."

"Well, hell's bells, boy," Artie replied. "An old man can't be expected to think of everything!"

Celie had a list as long as her arm.

Church: *check*. Minister: *check*. Reception hall: *check*. Invitations: *check*. Flowers: *check*. Cake: *check*. Wedding dress: *check*. Bridesmaids' dresses: *check*.

Maybe it was as long as both her arms.

She had memorized the wedding planner. She knew the symbolic meaning of every flower, of the candles, of the wedding rings. She knew type fonts and alternate wordings and parchment colors.

Sometimes she wished she hadn't bothered. It had been important before—the first time. With Matt. In fact, the wedding had mattered more than Matt.

Nothing mattered more than Jace.

But it was too late to back out now. Everything was rolling. They'd been home a month. She'd set the ball in motion immediately. She had her dress. She'd ordered her bouquet. She'd bought her veil. She'd chosen the bridesmaids' dresses. She arranged for the flowers. She'd picked out a cake. Just this morning she'd addressed the last of the invitations, and half an hour ago she'd stuck them in the mail.

She could hardly say, "Let's just elope, shall we?"

Though if she did, she had no doubt that Jace would instantly say, "Yes!"

Jace was no fan of big weddings. That was evident. He'd steered clear of all the planning. He'd said, "Whatever you want." He'd only asked that Artie be his best man. The rest, he'd said was up to her.

He had put up with a lot, and Celie knew it. Not just the wedding plans, but her insistence that he go back to Artie's every night, too.

"We've already slept together," he'd reminded her.

"Yes," she'd agreed. "But that was there. On the ship. It wasn't Elmer." It mattered somehow that they didn't scandalize Elmer. "You know Alice and Cloris... And what would Artie think?"

Artie, Jace had assured her, would think he was insane to be spending every night at his place.

But he did it. Every night for the past month he'd trekked back up the hill to sleep at Artie's. Celie had watched him make a point of waving to Alice and Cloris on his way.

"Reckon I'll get to wear white at the wedding?" he'd said last night on his way out the door.

Celie had laughed and kissed him. "Absolutely. And a halo, too."

"God knows I deserve it."

Celie thought he did, too.

The wedding was two weeks away when Polly called and asked them to come up to the ranch for the weekend.

"Sloan will be home," Celie said as she put a salad on the table for dinner. "He's coming back from Hong Kong tonight. And then sometime next week he's going to begin shooting his next film in Mexico."

"And you want to go see Sloan?" Jace said just a little warily.

But Celie shook her head. "I want to see them all. And *Polly* wants to see you. I don't think she still believes we're going to get married."

Jace, who had been counting the hours for what seemed like forever, sometimes didn't believe it, either. But there were under four hundred hours left now—and it was beginning to feel more believable.

"She would have come down to visit before now," Celie went on, "but she's been on her own up there with the kids while Sloan has been gone, and she hasn't had time. So, what do you say? Do you want to go?"

"A better question is—can you tear yourself away from preparations?"

"For a weekend," Celie said, "yes, I think so. There are several last-minute things to do. But we still have time."

"Too much time," Jace muttered. But maybe going up to Polly and Sloan's would make the hours pass faster. He hoped.

He picked Celie up bright and early Saturday morning. He had no reason to stay in bed, after all.

"Not for another 335 hours or so. Unless—" he looked hopefully at her "—we're sharing a room at Polly's?"

Celie shrugged. "It's up to Polly."

Jace understood that. He hoped his future sister-in-law felt kindly toward him. She had, he reminded Celie, let Sloan spend the night in her house in Elmer. She hadn't sent him up the hill to sleep at Artie's.

"No, he slept in the Jack's bottom bunk," Celie informed him.

Oh.

Jace tried not to think about it. He tried not to think about Celie sitting so close to him. Tried not to remember how good she'd felt in his arms. How good she'd felt naked.

"Tell me about these wedding plans," he said desperately. That had to be as deadly as naming presidents or reciting multiplication tables.

Celie told him about the reception. She detailed the menu. She talked about the music. She told him about the flowers, about the symbolic meaning of each one. She talked about the wedding cake, about the bridesmaids' dresses, about her own.

"It's gorgeous." She turned shining eyes on him. "You're going to love it."

Jace nodded. She could wear a sack as far as he was concerned. In fact he thought he'd prefer a sack. "I'll love it," he assured her, "only if it doesn't have a lot of little buttons."

Celie laughed. "It doesn't. Well, only forty or fifty or so."

Jace groaned.

She told him he still needed to go to Bozeman to be fitted for his tux. She hadn't given up on the tux idea, no matter how long he'd put it off.

"You need to take Artie, too," she told him. "And the rest of the men. You'll need five."

"Five? What for?"

"Ushers. Groomsmen."

Jace could just see himself talking five of his buddies into wearing tuxes. It didn't bear thinking about.

"The only one you don't have to worry about is Sloan," Celie told him.

That was news to him. Sloan was the only one he'd ever worried about.

"Why not?"

"He has a tux of his own."

Oh. Right. They were talking about tuxes. And Celie would know that Sloan had one, too, because she'd been to a Hollywood premiere with him.

Far from not worrying about Sloan Gallagher, Jace felt suddenly like punching his soon-to-be brother-in-law in the nose.

The feeling lasted until they got to the ranch.

But there, once Sloan and Polly came out to meet them, the feeling evaporated. He could see how happy Sloan had made Polly—and how happy Polly had made Sloan. He could also see that Celie was equally happy for both of them.

Given that, he couldn't really resent Sloan's single weekend in Celie's life. But he couldn't quite forgive the man for having his own tux.

"Oh, I can't believe it! You're getting married!" Polly swooped down the steps and ran toward them, then enveloped them both in a fierce hug.

Jace thought his ribs might crack.

Then Polly stood back and looked them up and down, still beaming. "Look at you! You both look so happy!" She shook her head as if it amazed her.

As well it might, considering the way Celie used to snarl at him and he used to tease her. Now he just grinned and Celie did, too.

"They are happy, Pol'," Sloan said, looping his arm over his wife's shoulders. "Almost as happy as we are."

"Impossible," Polly said. Then she said, "Come see the house and meet our guests. Sloan brought his work home with him." She slipped out from under Sloan's arm and grabbed Celie's hand and led her toward the house, leaving Sloan with Jace.

Once upon a time as hot-headed teenagers, the two of them had battered each other into the dirt. Jace had broken Sloan's nose. A week later Sloan had returned the favor.

Jace couldn't even remember why they'd been at odds then. Six months ago he had been flat out jealous.

He'd done everything wrong—from teasing her about her crush on a movie star to trying to make her jealous in return by flirting with every girl who came in the hardware store to inviting three of them, including starlet Tamara Lynd, to staying at Artie's with him to goading Celie into bidding on "the man of her dreams" at the auction.

Of course he'd hoped she'd see the folly of her ways. He'd never expected her to actually bid enough to win Sloan! He'd been floored—and furious—when she had. And he'd done something even stupider afterward.

Not that she'd noticed what he was doing. She'd only had eyes for Sloan. She'd come home from Hollywood after her weekend there and had let him think she was still madly in love with Sloan.

Thinking about it could still make him simmer.

Now he looked at Sloan and wondered what the other man was thinking.

Then Sloan drawled, "So I guess congratulations are in order." A wry grin touched his face. He stuck out his hand for Jace to shake.

For just a moment Jace hesitated, feeling awkward even though he knew he had no reason. Polly and Sloan were happy. They were in love.

In fact, Celie said, he'd been in love with Polly for years. And she'd said it without any kind of sadness, just very matter-of-fact, as if she really was over Sloan. She certainly hadn't hung around looking goopy-eyed at him. She'd gone off with Polly quite happily.

"You're not sure?" Sloan's grin faded as he misinterpreted Jace's hesitation.

"I'm sure," Jace said flatly. He gripped Sloan's hand and shook it. Hard. Their eyes met.

"You do love her," Sloan said quietly.

It wasn't a question, but Jace answered it anyway. "Yes."

The grin tipped the corner of Sloan's mouth again. "Good. She deserves that. She's had a rough time," he reflected after a moment.

Jace supposed that Polly had probably told him about Matt. Jace didn't think Celie had.

He nodded. "Yes."

"She blamed you."

Jace sighed. "Yes."

Sloan's hard blue gaze bored into him. "Did she have a right to?"

For years Jace would have said no. He'd have said he'd done her a favor, that if Matt Williams wasn't ready to settle down it was better to know before the wedding than after. And that was true. But…

Now he shifted from one foot to the other. His gaze wavered a moment, then came back to meet Sloan's. "I'd like to say no."

But he couldn't. Not honestly. He could have behaved better. He could have been a better example. He could have acted more grown-up and responsible himself.

Sloan's mouth twisted wryly. His gaze dropped for a moment, too. Then he looked up again and nodded. "We should all have no regrets."

Jace knew they were both remembering the foolish fight they'd had. The broken noses and battle scars were probably only small regrets compared to some of the stupid things they'd done over the past twenty years.

"I'm a better man now," Jace vowed, and hoped it was true.

Sloan looked toward the ranch house that his wife and her sister had just entered. "For their sakes," he said, still smiling, though his eyes were serious, "let's hope we both are."

"Jace, I'd like you to meet Gavin McConnell." Polly drew Jace into the wood-paneled living room of the Gallagher ranch house, which was crawling with people. Four of them were Polly's kids. He barely had time to get a look at the others as she turned to the lean, dark-haired man standing by the fireplace who had his arm looped over Celie's shoulders.

"Gavin, this is Jace Tucker. Gavin's an actor," Polly said to Jace. And to Gavin, she said, "Jace is a horse trainer. And Celie's fiancé," she announced proudly.

Calling Gavin McConnell "an actor" was like calling Babe Ruth a baseball player. Even Jace, who was by no means a movie buff, knew his name and the rugged, hard, handsome face that went with it. Gavin McConnell was famous. The characters he played were always memorable, and his films were guaranteed smash hits. He had won two Academy Awards and had at least two more nominations.

He was, according to the Sunday supplements and popular press, a "man's man," an "actor's actor" and "every woman's dream."

And right now he had his arm around Celie.

He was also sticking out his other hand to Jace and saying, "Congratulations! That's great. Celie's a great gal."

"Yeah," Jace said, suppressing the instinct to add, *my*

gal. He was fairly sure Celie wouldn't be impressed by his caveman instincts. He shook McConnell's hand and did his best to behave in a way that would reflect well on the Tucker name. "Pleased to meet you. Heard a lot about you."

"I hope not." Gavin McConnell grimaced. And Jace remembered that besides being all those other things, McConnell was reputed to be something of a recluse, as well; at least, he didn't give many interviews gladly. He seemed to be willing to spend time with friends, though.

"You're workin' on a new film with Sloan?" Jace asked, remembering that Celie had said something about a couple of Sloan's fellow actors coming for the weekend to go over material before they started shooting down in Mexico.

"Yeah. It's my baby." Gavin grinned. "Sloan's starring. I'm directing."

"And I'm costarring," a bright, oddly familiar female voice cut in.

Jace turned around and blinked as a woman with long, dark hair crossed the room toward him, a wide happy smile on her face. It took him a moment to realize why the voice was so familiar. Her hair hadn't been long when he'd last seen her. It hadn't been dark, either.

"Oh, Jace," Polly said, "you remember Tamara Lynd, don't you?"

He hid out with Polly's kids.

He had no other alternative. Polly and Celie were immersed in wedding discussions that Jace wanted no part of. The words "formal attire" and "rehearsal dinner" made him shudder and head for the hills.

But he couldn't hang around with Sloan and Gavin and Tamara, either. And not just because they were "talking shop." They were going over the script, working out motivations, Gavin told him. Discussing their characters, talking about interaction, going on about the impact of past history. They all said he was welcome to listen in if he wanted.

He didn't—because he had no desire to dredge up past history.

Even more than *morning suit* and *tuxedo,* the words *past history* sent a nervous shiver up Jace's spine.

He had a bit of "past history" with Tamara Lynd. Meaningless history as far as he was concerned. Stupid history. History he very much wanted to forget.

He didn't know what Tamara thought about it—or what she might be inclined to do. She had a history of chasing men. She'd chased him.

And caught him—once—in a weak moment.

He wasn't weak right now. He wasn't susceptible anymore. But even so, the last thing he needed was Tamara hitting on him now.

So he kept his distance. He would have trailed Celie around like a sheepdog, but all those wedding plans drove him crazy. So he took refuge with the kids, spending hours in the corral with fourteen-year-old Daisy, helping her work out some kinks in the horse she was training and giving young Jack pointers on his riding so the boy could beat Eric, Sloan's foreman's grandson, when they raced.

He borrowed one of Sloan's horses and raced Jack a few times himself. It felt good to be back in the saddle. It felt right. It felt safe.

And then he turned around and saw Tamara and Gavin and Polly's very pregnant daughter, Sara, standing by the fence watching as he and Jack came back.

"You were wonderful!" Tamara exclaimed. She looked at Jace with shining eyes. "Wasn't he wonderful?" she demanded of the other two.

"You don't mean me, I s'pose?" Jack said.

Tamara grinned up at him. "You were wonderful, too,"

she told him. "You both were. It's just so…exciting… watching men ride. Isn't it?" She turned eagerly to Gavin and Sara.

"I'd rather watch women ride," Gavin said with a grin.

"I'd rather ride than watch," Sara said a little wistfully.

Another time Jace would have seized on that and offered to take her. It would have got him away from Tamara. But Sara was very pregnant—almost eight months—and Jace wasn't quite the rip-roaring cowboy who didn't think ahead that he used to be.

"I'll take you after the baby's born," he offered. "Come on out to the barn while I cool this horse down, and tell me what's been goin' on in your life."

If Sara was surprised at the invitation, she didn't say so. Instead she willingly waddled along with him toward the barn, talking about her pregnancy, about the college courses she was going to take in the spring if she could find the time, about not having given up her hope of going to medical school.

Jace listened. He admired Sara's fortitude, her commitment, her determination. He didn't know or care if Tamara was watching him. He didn't look back.

He couldn't avoid her entirely, though. They all ate together in the evening around the huge oak table in the dining room. Polly, aided by Celie when she could tear herself away from her plans and her lists, cooked enormous, wonderful meals. And afterwards, they all sat around the living room and told stories—about movies, about cowboying, about places they'd been and things they'd done.

Jace held back at first, standing in the doorway listening to the tales, worried that if he went in and sat down, Tamara might decide to come sit beside him. Celie had gone back to her lists and he was on his own. But Tamara barely gave him more than a grin and a glance as he stood there. She was regaling them all with a very funny story about a Paris fashion show she'd been in during the earliest days of her career.

"I didn't know you'd been a model." Gavin looked surprised.

"I was a terrible one. I wanted to be in show business, so I had to get noticed, be a star. And I had good bones—" she shrugged "—so I tried. But I also had two left feet. You need to be able to walk without looking down to be a runway model. They fired me after I fell off the runway!" She laughed and shook her head. "But it was a start. And I'd have done anything then to get my career going. A girl's gotta do what a girl's gotta do."

Even buy Sloan Gallagher, Jace thought. Her career had been stalled in the supporting-role stage last winter. She'd been doing backup roles—nasty other women, girls who died halfway through—for the past five years. She wasn't getting any younger, and she still had the dream. She'd been desperate for a boost. So she'd come to Elmer last winter to be noticed—to get media attention by winning Sloan Gallagher.

But she hadn't won. Celie had.

She'd been upset that day. Disgruntled. Annoyed. But philosophical. A girl did what a girl had to do, but she didn't win 'em all. Tamara knew that.

So she'd moved on that very night—to Jace.

That hadn't been to benefit her career, of course. That had been to assuage her pride. But in an odd twist of fate and serendipity, exactly what she'd hoped for had come to pass, anyway.

Indy film director John Cunningham had seen her in a news feature on Elmer. He'd said she looked haggard and desperate, not at all the way she'd come across in her films. He'd called her in Los Angeles three days later to see if she would be interested in playing the brittle spinster sister in his new film.

"And much to his surprise," Tamara said now, finishing the story, "he discovered I could act."

"Amen to that." Gavin said fervently. "I tapped her for Sloan's costar as soon as I saw some film."

Tamara beamed, first at Sloan and then at Celie, who had just come into the room. "Moral of the story—sometimes losing is winning." Then her gaze went from Celie to Jace and she gave him a broad wink. "Looks like it happened to you, too."

Celie looked at him a little curiously, but Jace breathed a little easier after that.

Tamara didn't have designs on him. She knew he was in love with Celie. She was happy for them both. She understood. She even spent time with Celie and Polly whenever Gavin gave her and Sloan a break, offering her opinion on wedding plans, saying how handsome Jace would look in a tux, and hoping out loud that she'd get invited to the wedding.

Jace didn't say anything to that.

Celie said, "Well, of course you will."

Later that night in bed—they actually had a room together because Gavin was sleeping in the bottom bunk in Jack's—Celie said, "Tamara's different than I thought she'd be. I mean, she's beautiful and opinionated and, I suppose you'd say...sexy...but she's real. I like Tamara. Don't you?"

"Sure," Jace said. "She's okay."

He didn't care one way or another about Tamara. He had other things on his mind—another *woman* on his mind.

"Come here," he muttered, hauling Celie close. "I need to love you."

They had a cookout Sunday afternoon. Afterward Celie and Jace packed up the truck and got ready to drive back to Elmer. In the morning a private plane would come to take Gavin and Sloan and Tamara to Mexico.

"Everybody's leavin'," Jack grumbled. "Don't see why we can't go, too."

"School," Polly said.

Jack wasn't impressed. "Who needs school?"

"You," Sloan told his stepson. "So you can grow up to be smart like me and your uncle Jace."

"Oh, yes," Polly said, rolling her eyes. "You two are such sterling examples of the well-educated man."

"They are good men," Tamara said with broad smile at both Sloan and Jace. Then she leaned up to give Jace a kiss goodbye. "They are wonderful men." Then she lowered her voice so the children wouldn't hear and added with a wicked grin, "And excellent lovers."

"Tam!" Sloan looked apoplectic.

Jace stood stock-still, too stunned to say a word.

"It's true," Tamara defended herself. "I was only saying. And I am speaking in past tense, of course." She patted Sloan's arm as if to reassure him, then turned her gaze on Polly and Celie.

"I never sleep with married men," she informed them cheerfully. "I never even tempt them," she added with a note of regret. "Not even really scrumptious men like these two."

Nine

It was like waiting for the other shoe to drop.

Jace told himself it could have been worse.

Tamara could have said he was a lousy lover. She could have tried to insinuate herself into his life again. She could have wrapped herself around him and declared he was hers, all hers. But clearly she wasn't any more interested in that than he was.

He just hoped Celie understood that.

He wished she would say something.

They'd driven miles—they were almost back in Elmer, for heaven's sake—and she hadn't said a word.

Well, no, that wasn't quite true. She'd said a few words. Whenever he'd asked a direct question, like, "Do you want to stop and get a cup of coffee?" or "Do you want to play a tape?" she'd said, "No, thanks," politely, even pleasantly. But her words had been distant, almost absentminded, as if she wasn't really there.

So where was she?

And what was she thinking?

He wondered if he should try to explain. But how did you go about telling the woman you loved about a night you'd spent with another woman?

How could he explain that Tamara meant nothing to him, that in fact, the night he'd slept with her it had been because Celie had spent her life's savings on a date with another man? A man who had a damn sight more to recommend him than Jace did in every way.

He spent miles trying to find the right words, rehearsing them in his mind. But every time he did, the words stuck in his throat.

Sleeping with Tamara Lynd had been immature, stupid and consummate bad sportsmanship. If everything else Celie had ever thought about him over the past ten years had painted him in a bad light, telling her this wasn't going to help matters. It would be like giving her evidence to hang him.

So he kept his mouth shut. About that.

He talked heartily, almost frantically, about what a good time he'd had over the weekend, about what a good guy Sloan had turned out to be and what a nice, down-to-earth guy Gavin McConnell was. And because naturally he had to say something about Tamara, too, or Celie would have known he was avoiding talking about her, he said he thought she'd put on a little weight.

"You'd know," Celie said.

Damn. He should have kept his big mouth shut. Quickly, desperately, he changed the subject to Sara. "Speaking of people who've gained weight..."

Jace always talked fast when he was nervous. He talked a lot when he was nervous. He babbled about how impressed he was with Sara's determination to keep on with her studies, about how smart she was, about how she was making the best of a difficult situation. "She's a good kid," he said when he finally had to pause for breath.

"Yes." Celie stared at the mountains out the side window of his pickup. She didn't say anything else.

Jace drummed his fingers on the steering wheel. He cracked his knuckles. He fidgeted and shot sidelong glances at Celie. She didn't look his way. She didn't say a word.

Say something, he begged her silently. *Ask me what happened!*

Hell, she could even yell at him, if she wanted to. It would be better than this.

But the silence continued.

"So," he said finally as they were approaching Elmer, "did you and Polly get all the wedding plans sorted out? Is everything set?"

"Hmm? Oh, I guess."

"Great. I can hardly wait to drag Artie in to try on a tux." Jace grinned as he pulled up in front of Polly's old house.

Celie smiled faintly. Jace cut the engine and jumped out. Celie was already getting out by the time he came around to her side of the truck. He grabbed her bag out of the topper and followed her up the steps.

She opened the door and took the bag from him. "Thanks. Bye."

"It's not late. Cloris and Alice would let me come in."

"We've been gone two days. You better go check on Artie." She didn't meet his eyes.

Jace felt anxiety swirling through him. "Artie's fine."

She was shutting him out and he had to do something, even the last thing he wanted to do. "Celie, look," he said desperately, "we need to talk."

"I need to think."

"No. You don't! Not about what Tamara said, I mean. We're not—we haven't— Well, once we did,' he admitted.

"But it didn't mean anything. It's over. It isn't ever going to happen again! I swear."

Celie nodded. "I believe you."

"You do?" He stared at her. He gulped. "I mean, of course you do! Good! Great. Thank God!"

A huge wave of relief swamped him. He grinned, though his heart was still slamming and his knees were still wobbling. "So you...understand? She doesn't mean anything to me. It was a one-off. One night. One stupid night."

She nodded again, but she wasn't smiling. She was looking thoughtful.

"Celie?"

She smiled and patted his hand. "I understand," she said.

Did she? Oh, God, he hoped.

Celie understood perfectly.

She'd been a fool. It had just taken Tamara Lynd to open her eyes.

She thought about it all night. She paced the house, twisting Jace's ring on her finger, pressing the diamond between her tight lips and feeling sick.

And in the morning she got up and went to the hardware store before it opened. She wanted to see Jace alone before Artie got there.

He was stacking boxes. And when she opened the door, he turned around and, at the sight of her, a grin lit his face.

Celie steeled her heart against it. She couldn't do this if she let herself fall under his spell.

He hurried toward her. "Hey! You're out early."

She smiled, knowing it didn't reach her eyes. She held out her hand. "I came to give you something. Here."

He stared at her clenched bare, ringless fingers, and then at her face. He shoved his hands in his pockets and shook his head. "No."

"What do you mean, no? Go on, Jace, take it." She thrust it at him again. Her gaze met his for only an instant, then shied away. "It's yours. I'm giving it back."

But he kept his hands right where they were and shook his head. "Why? You said you believed me!" Fierce blue eyes challenged her.

"I do believe you," Celie told him. She kept trying to push the ring at him.

But Jace backed away. "Then why are you doing this?"

"Because I can't...I can't marry you!"

He shook his head. "Why not? She doesn't mean anything to me. It was past. You said you understood. Celie, come on. It doesn't make any sense!"

"It does to me." She wrapped her arms across her chest. She rocked back and forth, the pain of her realization emanating from the very depths of her soul.

"Then explain it to me."

She wet her lips, took a breath, held it, then exhaled with a shudder. "It won't work," she said finally.

Jace's brows drew down. "What do you mean, it won't work? What won't work?"

"Our marriage. You and me!" The pain was welling up now, tearing at her. "It won't work. How can it? I wasn't even enough for Matt!" she said, anguished, and turned away.

"*What?*" Jace stared at her, poleaxed. He came after her, grabbed her arms and turned her to face him. "Matt? What the hell does Matt have to do with this?"

"You slept with Tamara!"

"The more fool me," Jace said bitterly. "Yeah, I did. One time. The night you bought Sloan at the auction. I was a wreck. I was angry. I was bitter. I wanted—hell, I don't know what I wanted!" He raked a hand through his hair. "I was starin' out the window, lookin' down at your place and wonderin' what the hell had possessed you. And Ta-

mara came to my room and said there were more fish in
the sea. So I had sex with her. It wasn't exactly memorable.
In fact, it was lousy!''

Celie stared at him. She tried to digest that, to see it as
Jace had seen it. But when she had, it made no difference.

''Exactly,'' she said softly.

Jace looked at her, uncomprehending. ''Huh?''

''It was lousy, you said.''

''What?''

''You knew!''

He looked baffled. ''Knew what?''

''That it was lousy! You had comparisons. You could
judge. You could tell the difference. And you'll…you'll be
able to tell about me!'' Celie pulled out of his grasp and
walked away, then turned to face him. ''It's not about Tamara, Jace,'' she admitted in a low voice. ''It's about me.
I wasn't enough even for Matt who didn't know anything.
You've been with lots of women. You've slept with Tamara Lynd. I can't compete with that.''

''I love you, damn it!''

Celie swallowed. ''Now,'' she said. ''Now you think you
do.''

''I do,'' Jace said just as stubbornly.

But she didn't accept that. ''It's not real. It was, like
Simone said, a shipboard romance. It won't last.''

''Of course it will last.''

''No. It won't. You thought you had this thing for me
for a long time. It's just a matter of pursuit. The thrill of
the hunt, the joy of the chase.'' She'd thought about it all
night. ''I was like the fish in the lake that you couldn't
catch, so you kept coming back until you did.''

Jace was shaking his head, staring at her, a dazed look
on his face.

''But then you caught me. And you're happy. You think

you've got what you want. And you do. For now. But it's not enough for fifty years.''

Jace said something very rude that made Celie blink. Then he said, ''I don't believe I'm hearing this.''

''It's true, Jace. Once you've had me, you'll be ready to move on. You've had other women. You've had Tamara—''

''I never loved any other woman!''

''I won't be enough for you. I can't be,'' she said. And as much as she hated to admit it, that was the bottom-line truth. She couldn't marry him and then fail him. It would be worse than not marrying him at all.

For a long minute Jace didn't speak. He stared at her, at his feet, at the ceiling, then back at her again.

''So it all comes back to Matt, does it?'' he said quietly. ''You loved him that much?''

''No,'' Celie said. ''I didn't! I don't! I thought I loved him. But I loved the idea of getting married. He was just…just the reason.''

''And me? Was I just another reason?'' Jace said bitterly.

''Of course not!''

Fierce eyes bored into her. ''So you love me?''

''It's not about love, '' Celie argued, avoiding his question.

''Yes, it is,'' Jace insisted. ''It's only about love. I love you, damn it, Celie O'Meara. And I'm not going to get tired of you in fifty years or even a hundred and fifty, if we have that long.''

''We won't,'' Celie said.

''We might.''

''Stop it, Jace!'' She thrust the ring at him again. ''Here. Take it.''

He pulled his hands out of his pockets, but he didn't reach out and take the ring. Instead he folded his arms across his chest. "No. I'm not going to take it. I asked you to marry me and you said yes."

"And now I'm saying no."

"Too bad."

She frowned. "What do you mean, too bad?"

"The wedding is scheduled."

"We'll call it off."

"No, I won't."

"Then I will."

"You made a promise. You promised to marry me."

"I'll fail you!" There! She'd said it.

But Jace just shook his head. "No. You won't. I believe in you. I believe in our commitment. Don't you?"

"I'm a realist, Jace."

"You're a coward."

Her lips pressed tightly together as she absorbed the blow. "Maybe I am," she allowed. "So take back the ring. You don't want to marry a coward."

"I want to marry you, Celie. And I'm not taking back the ring. I gave it to you in good faith. You accepted it. I'm going ahead with the wedding. And if you don't want to get married, you know what you'll have to do—jilt me."

It was the most ridiculous thing she'd ever heard.

Who insisted on going ahead with a wedding if the bride said she wasn't going to show up?

Jace Tucker, that was who.

Stubborn, bullheaded trouble-making Jace!

Celie despaired of him. She was sorry—God only knew *how* sorry. But she knew, sorry or not, that she was right. She had been living in a dream world, believing that she would be able to keep up with Jace, satisfy Jace.

But it wasn't true.

How could she possibly keep a man like that interested in her? She hadn't even been able to hang on to Matt! And

Sloan! Sloan thought she was a nice girl, but he'd never been interested in her—only in Polly.

She'd gained some self-confidence over the past few months, but after she'd heard Tamara's words, her fledgling confidence had been dealt a death blow.

She was being sensible, practical, smart. She was saving them both a lifetime of misery, because there was no way on earth he could possibly be content with her for the rest of his life.

He'd gone to bed with Tamara Lynd, for heaven's sake!

And while she absolutely believed him when he said it had been a one-off and that he wasn't about to go to bed with Tamara again, that didn't mean he wouldn't be tempted by some other woman.

Of course he would be tempted, because there was nothing special or wonderful or astonishing about Celie O'Meara that would keep him home and content for the rest of his life.

He would get bored. He would want greener pastures. The fault wasn't his; it was hers. In the long run Celie didn't have the confidence in herself that she had what it took.

Jace was just too stubborn to see it. Yet.

He would, though. When she refused to see him, refused to talk to him, called the caterer and the florist and the minister, he'd realize she meant what she said.

And that would be the end of it.

"A tux?" Artie said doubtfully. He looked at Jace over the baling wire and shook his head. "I don't believe I've ever worn a tux."

"Me, neither," Jace said. "But it's what Celie wants. So we're going after work this afternoon to get fitted."

He'd called the place in Bozeman Celie had mentioned and told them he'd be in. He'd called Noah and Taggart and Gus, too, and told them to get over there and get fitted. He didn't put up with any arguments. He'd moaned and groaned himself. Now he was just going for it.

"Got a suit," Artie went on. "Navy blue serge. Bought it when me an' Maudie got married."

Which would make it sixty-odd years old, Jace thought. "We'll bury you in it, Artie. You're wearing a tux for the wedding."

Artie looked at him with surprise. "Gettin' mighty bossy, ain't you?"

Getting mighty desperate, that was the truth of the matter.

He'd called the minister this morning to make sure everything was set for a week from Saturday.

"Who is this?" the minister sounded surprised. "Jace Tucker? But I thought—Celie said—"

"Celie's just panickin' a little," Jace said. "Hold the date. Hold the time. We'll be there."

He ended up having to do the same with Poppy about the flowers, with Denise, the caterer, with Julie Ann, who was making the cake.

"Celie canceled," Poppy told him about the flowers, Denise told him about the meal, Julie Ann told him about the cake.

And to every one of them Jace said, "No. It's on. We'll be there." And when Julie Ann had sounded doubtful, he'd promised her a check.

"You'll make the cake if you get paid, right?"

"Yes, but—"

"Fine. I'll bring you a check."

Just to make sure, he paid the caterer, too. And the organist for the church. He also sent Polly a check payable to the Elmer Town Fund for rent of the town hall.

She called him when she got it. "What are you doing? Celie said the wedding is off."

"It's not off," Jace said firmly.

"Oh? Well, good. I wondered if the Tamara thing would give her cold feet."

"She, um, got a little nervous," Jace said.

"Well, it was in the past." Polly gave him the benefit of the doubt. "Just like Sloan's experience with her. And I can tell you *that* won't happen again!"

Jace believed her. There was no way Sloan was going to stray from a woman like Polly. There was no way he'd ever stray from Celie.

He loved her and he always would.

He just hoped that by October third at 3:00 p.m., Celie believed it, too.

It was the most bizarre thing in the world.

Celie had called off the wedding—and no one believed her.

She'd phoned the caterer, the florist, the minister, the organist, the baker—everyone who had anything to do with the plans she'd made. She'd told them it was off. And they'd all said they were very sorry to hear it.

And the next day the baker had called and asked if she wanted raspberries on the cake.

"There is no cake," Celie said. "There isn't going to be a wedding."

"Right, Jace said you'd say that," Julie Ann said soothingly. "Don't worry, it's just nerves."

"It's *not* nerves!" Celie insisted.

"Fine. Do you want raspberries or not?" Julie Ann persisted.

"If Jace arranged this," Celie practically shouted, "ask Jace!"

She did the same thing when the caterer called and asked whether to serve baby carrots or green beans. She did the same when the organist wanted her to narrow down the music choices for the wedding.

"Ask Jace," she said, ready to pull out her hair. "Just ask Jace!"

The banging on the door startled Artie. He frowned and dropped his fork. "What in tarnation...?"

Jace, who had a fairly good idea who was doing the banging, pushed himself away from the table and stood up. "I'll take care of it."

It was, just as he'd thought, Celie fuming and pacing on the porch. She rounded on him when he opened the door. "Exactly what do you think you're doing?" she demanded.

He dabbed at his lips with his napkin. "Eatin' dinner?"

She made a furious explosive sound. "With Poppy! With Julie Ann! With the minister!"

"Just firmin' things up," Jace said easily, admiring the high color in her cheeks. "I told Julie Ann yes to the raspberries. I always liked raspberries. I said green beans rather than carrots, but if you want—"

"I don't want! I don't care! I'm *not* marrying you!"

"Sure you are, Cel'. You got to. You love me."

But she wished she didn't. Oh, God, how she wished!

It was because she loved him that she wouldn't marry him, damn it. It was because she didn't want to fail him, to hurt him, to *bore* him for the rest of his life, for goodness' sakes!

He didn't realize how boring she was. She hadn't really realized it until she'd compared herself with Tamara. That had been a wake-up call, all right.

It had awakened every dormant insecurity Celie had ever known.

She had bid on Sloan, yes. And that had been a brave, daring—let's face it, desperate—thing to do. But all her weekend with Sloan had done was prove that she had good taste in men. It hadn't proved that a man like Sloan could love her.

On the contrary, he loved Polly, who was everything she was not. Polly was tough and clever and capable. Polly had always faced the world head-on, had dared to do things that Celie wouldn't dare in a million lifetimes.

She was the right sort of woman for Sloan. She—or Tamara or some other woman—was undoubtedly the right woman for Jace.

But Jace—stupid Jace!—didn't believe that!

He thought she was some daring, adventurous woman who went sailing off into the sunset. In fact, nothing was further from the truth.

She might have sailed off into a few sunsets just recently, but she'd had to make herself do it. They'd been memorable, but no more memorable than the sunsets she'd seen on Jace and his sister's ranch when they'd come home. She'd visited half a dozen foreign ports, too, and she was glad she had. But they hadn't captivated her, either. No more than life in Elmer did. She was every bit the boring provincial girl Armand had always believed she was.

How could Jace Tucker, who had been to bed with Tamara Lynd and heaven knew how many other enticing women, possibly want to spend the rest of his life with the most boring woman on earth?

He could get a job as a wedding consultant, Jace figured, by the time this was all over. And he might have to if he had to get out of town because he'd become the laughing-stock of the entire Shields Valley.

It was a possibility—because as time went on, he found that Celie was being just as stubborn as he was.

After their battle on Artie's front porch, from which

she'd stomped away, furious, she had avoided him every-where.

He'd gone into the grocery store the following day as she was checking out. She had turned her back on him and kept right on talking to Carol Ferguson.

"Hey, Cel'," he'd said. "How ya doin', Carol?"

Carol had talked to him, had chatted a bit. Celie had pretended he wasn't even there.

The next day Julie Ann had called him to ask about the cake topper.

"The what?" Jace was mystified.

"The bit that sits on top," Julie Ann explained. "Celie didn't know what she wanted before. And she won't say now. She says it's your wedding, ask you." Julie Ann seemed to think this was very odd behavior, but dutifully she asked, "So take your pick. You can have a bride and groom, a dove of peace or wedding bells."

He should probably pick the dove of peace, Jace thought. It was clearly what they needed. But even more than that he needed a bride. "The bride and groom," he told Julie Ann.

At least that way one would be there.

"Celie ticked at you?" Artie asked him the Wednesday before the wedding when Jace came home for lunch.

Jace had deliberately not said anything to Artie about Celie's change of heart. He knew Artie. Artie would have a solution. And the last thing he needed right now was a ninety-year-old know-it-all telling him what to do.

"She's just gettin' nervous," Jace answered.

Artie nodded as he slapped ham on bread and slathered mustard on top. "I'll say," he agreed. "Told me she wasn't marryin' you."

So much for circumspection. "What'd I tell you? Nerves," Jace said, trying to sound calm.

Artie stuck another piece of bread on top of the ham,

whacked through it with the butcher knife and handed Jace the sandwich. "You sure it's just nerves?"

"Of course I'm sure."

"So we're still gonna wear them tuxes?" Artie, for all his grousing, seemed to be looking forward to his tux.

"We're going to wear the tuxes," Jace said firmly. "That's what I told her."

Ho, boy. Jace raised his brows, imagining Celie's reaction to that. "And she said?"

"Didn't say nothin'. Just got all red in the face and sort of steamy lookin'. That's what made me think she was ticked at you."

"How can you lie to that defenseless old man?" Celie's voice was shrill on the phone against his ear.

"Huh?" Jace had been expecting Taggart to call back about some lumber. He straightened up now, hearing Celie instead. His heart began beating double time. "Hey, Cel'. How are you?"

"Don't you 'Hey, Cel' me! Why haven't you told Artie?"

"Told him what?"

"You know very well what! He still thinks the wedding is on."

"It is."

"It's not! You know it's not. You're going to look like a fool."

Jace paused. "Maybe I will," he said slowly. "I guess that's up to you."

Celie was sitting by herself in the kitchen listening to the clock tick and scratching Sid the cat's ears when she heard footsteps on the porch.

Whoever was at the door, she wasn't answering it.

She didn't want to see anyone, didn't want to talk to

anyone. Didn't want to tell one more person that no, she wasn't going to marry Jace Tucker tomorrow even though he was telling everyone she was!

"They can just go away," she told Sid, who scraped his jaw against her ankle and butted her calf with his head. "We don't need anyone, do we?"

But before Sid could respond, the door opened and Polly, Sara, Lizzie, Daisy and Jack all poured into the room, banging and talking and jostling.

"Hey, Aunt Celie!" Jack beamed at her.

"Hi, Aunt Celie!" Daisy and Lizzie chimed.

"Hi, Cel'," Polly said, "Got your dancin' shoes on?"

Celie just stared at them all. "What on earth are you doing here?"

"We came for the wedding," Sara said. The rest of them nodded.

"And tonight we're going to The Barrel," Polly said cheerfully.

"What?"

An evening spent at The Barrel bar down in Livingston near the date of a wedding was a tradition among local women and had been since World War II when a rancher's daughter, set to marry in the morning, had met a visiting sailor there and had run off with him instead.

"Tempting fate," they had called it ever after. Women who did it and went on to marry their chosen man had good marriages—or so the story went.

"I'm not getting married," Celie insisted.

The girls looked scandalized, Jack looked stunned.

Polly rolled her eyes. "You do whatever you want tomorrow, but I'm not missing a night at The Barrel. Get dressed. Let's go pick up Mom and Cait. Get those dancing shoes on!"

It was crazy, Celie thought. Insane. Ridiculous. How

could you go out to test fate against a man you were determined you weren't marrying?

But they went. The Barrel was loud, rocking, riotous and crowded as The Barrel usually was on Friday night. Not Celie's sort of place at all.

Jace had been here, though. Celie remembered that he'd rescued Sara last winter when she'd come here looking for a ride home. There were a hundred girls here more suited to Jace than she was. She wanted to go home.

"How about him?" Cait, her best friend from high school and now her stepsister, poked her in the ribs.

"What? Who?" Celie turned, baffled, "What are you talking about?"

"Him." Cait pointed to a hunky young cowboy wearing skin-tight stacked Wranglers and a hot-pink shirt. He was playing pool, bending over the table, giving them a very nice view. "We're supposed to be offering you alternatives to Jace," Cait reminded her.

"I don't need alternatives," Celie said. "I'm not marrying Jace."

"Or him." Felicity Jones nodded her head in the direction of another handsome man dancing with a hungry-looking female.

Celie shook her head and looked away. "Not interested."

They offered up half a dozen more—a stud playing Keno, two rodeo cowboys clearly just passing through, a dapper-looking gent with a handlebar mustache.

"There are some interesting specimens here," Polly said finally after she'd looked over the crowd. Then she looked at her sister. "But none quite as interesting as Jace."

Celie, whose traitorous mind had been thinking along the same lines, deliberately turned away.

She didn't want to compare Jace to the rest of Livingston's manhood. She already knew the verdict. He was better than all of them. Handsomer than all of them. More wonderful than all of them.

The problem wasn't what Jace was lacking, damn it!

The problem was her!

She felt like curling into a tiny ball of misery.

Polly touched her shoulder. "Come on. I think it's time we went home."

Jace had been to his fair share of stag nights.

He'd always laughed and joked and commiserated with the poor son of a gun who, in scant hours, would be relinquishing his freedom, trading his free rein for a double yoke.

Now on Friday night at the Dew Drop, his buddies held a stag night for him—and he could only hope that the woman he loved would be at his wedding.

"You sure you're ready for this?" Taggart teased him after he'd raised his glass in a toast. "Celie doesn't seem to be too thrilled."

"Celie's nervous," Jace said. "She got jilted once, remember."

Everyone remembered. There was a moment of silence as they stared into their beer and thought about that jerk Matt Williams.

Then Taggart shrugged. "Well, hell, man, you're not Matt. She oughta know you won't do that to her!"

"Right," Shane Nichols seconded it. And half a dozen local cowboys agreed.

And they were right. Jace wouldn't. Ever.

But it was looking very much like she was going to do it to him. She hadn't come around as he had hoped. She hadn't been bowled over by his determination. She hadn't come to tell him she was sorry, that he was right. She hadn't said she loved him.

He wasn't even sure now that she did.

Maybe for her it *had* been a shipboard romance.

Maybe he had swept her off her feet, made her giddy, caused her to dream—but only briefly. Maybe now that she was back in Elmer, her memories of the pain of the past meant more to her than he did.

She was still saying she wasn't going to marry him.

He was still insisting she was. It was just nerves, he'd told everyone. Celie was just remembering the past, remembering what had happened to her last time. And who could blame her? he'd said. But this time wasn't going to be like last time. Of course the wedding was still on. He'd see them at the church at three o'clock on Saturday.

"Here now. Time for a toast by the best man," Jace heard Artie say, and he turned to see the old man raise his glass. "To the best doggone feller I ever known," Artie said, "and to the gal I love like—" he faltered momentarily and cleared his throat "—like a granddaughter. I'm so glad they're gonna spend the rest of their lives makin' each other happy!"

Ten

"**S**he's not gonna do it, you know." Jace came and stood in the doorway to Artie's bedroom as the old man was just climbing into bed.

He had to say something, had to prepare Artie. He couldn't let him get all dressed up tomorrow and stand there at the front of the church next to Jace, expecting to see Celie walk down the aisle to meet them when she wasn't going to.

Jace swallowed past the hard lump in his throat and pressed on. "She isn't gonna marry me, Artie."

Artie turned from the bed slowly and straightened up again. "No?"

Jace shook his head. "'Fraid not." He mustered up a wan smile.

Artie wasn't fooled. "You love her."

Jace swallowed again. "Always. I'll always love her. But she—I don't know anymore. Maybe she doesn't really love me." It was hard to get the words out. He hunched his shoulders and bent his head.

"So what're you gonna do?" Artie asked.

Jace's faint smile turned wry. "You mean you're not going to tell me?"

Artie grinned just a little at the hit. "A feller doesn't live ninety years without learning a few things," he said. "Don't mean to boss you. I guess I just reckoned you could use a little hard-won wisdom."

"I still could," Jace admitted. "If I go there tomorrow and she doesn't come—"

It didn't bear thinking about. Yet maybe it was exactly what he deserved—a just revenge for whatever part he'd played in Matt's jilting her all those years ago. Was the world really that fair?

"Well now," Artie said. "Lemme tell you a little story." He sat on the bed and nodded toward the rocking chair.

Jace, knotting his fingers together, obediently sat down. Would it be zen this time? he wondered. Or some other self-help guru Artie had stumbled upon. It didn't matter, Jace decided. He just needed help.

"Long time ago," Artie said, "when I was younger than you are now, I met the girl of my dreams..." He leaned forward, rested his forearms on his knees and stared down at the braid rug beneath his feet.

So it wasn't going to be zen? It was going to be personal? The story of Artie's courtship of Maudie? Jace leaned forward, too.

"I was cowboyin' out in Washington State," Artie went on. "Big spread owned by a feller named Jack Carew. He had a couple a thousand head of Herefords, a ranch that run for miles into the sweetest country you can imagine, and the prettiest daughter you ever did see."

"Maudie?"

But Artie didn't reply. He went right on. "I fancied the

daughter somethin' fierce. But I was just a broke cowpoke workin' on her daddy's ranch. Didn't have nothin' to recommend me, that's for sure.''

"Except your charming personality," Jace said dryly.

Artie lifted his head. "Well, sure. 'Cept that." He gave Jace a faint grin and flexed his bony shoulders. "Turned out to be enough. Turned out she fancied me, too." The old man flushed slightly. "We had a, um...bit of a fling. Well, it wasn't a fling really. We was serious. And I asked her to marry me."

Jace nodded. And they'd lived happily ever after for fifty-odd years. So what did this have to do with him and Celie?

"She said yes. But her daddy said no. Said I couldn't support her the way she ought to be."

"I hope you told him to go to hell," Jace said.

Artie's mouth twisted. "Couldn't. He was right."

"But—"

The old man shrugged and bent his head again. "He was. She'd had pert much ever'thing she could want, includin' a college education. Her ol' man was right when he said she was wastin' her time on me."

"I didn't know Maudie had a college education."

Artie's head snapped up. "Will you stop talkin' an' start *listenin'* fer a change? I ain't talkin' about Maudie!"

Jace's mouth opened. And shut. He stared at Artie as if he'd never seen the old man before. Not Maudie? Then who—?

"She didn't care what I had," Artie went on, a faraway expression on his face. "Told me so. Told me she loved me an' all that didn't matter to her, that I just had to believe her." He sighed. "But I didn't."

He sat up straight and threw his shoulders back and stared straight ahead. "I was too worried her old man was right. Figured he had to be, him bein' so smart an' so successful an' all. She wanted me to run away with her. Told me we didn't need him. Didn't need anybody but each other. But I didn't believe her. I didn't want to get hurt. Didn't want to hurt her. So I played it safe," he said bitterly. "I quit an' I came back to Elmer. Didn't even tell her where I was goin'." He let out a sigh, then added almost as an afterthought, "Couple a years later I married Maudie."

And?

Jace just looked at him, trying to make the connections Artie expected him to make. Hell, this was harder than zen. He didn't say anything, just sat there trying to figure it out.

"I loved her," Artie said. "She loved me. I shoulda taken the risk."

"You don't know that," Jace said. "It might not have lasted."

Artie met his gaze. "It lasted," he said simply.

Jace shook his head, disbelieving. "But…but Maudie…you and Maudie…"

Artie sighed and rubbed a hand over the wisps of white hair on his head. "I loved Maudie. I was faithful to Maudie. Always. Even after Anna came…"

"Anna? That was her name? She came? To Elmer?"

"Tracked me down," Artie said, his gaze still faraway. "Took her three years. Daddy wasn't inclined to tell her where I'd come from, and I never had. But she was stubborn and determined. She still loved me," he said wistfully. "An' she brung somethin' to show me." His gaze came back to meet Jace's. "Our daughter."

"Daughter? You had a—" Jace felt as if he'd been punched.

"Have," Artie corrected. He smiled faintly. "Still have. She doesn't know."

"But you do? You keep track—" Jace was floundering. "Where—?"

"Here. She's here," Artie replied. "Always has been... ever since. It's Joyce."

Jace stared. *Joyce? Celie's mother?*

"Then you...you're...you're Celie's *grandfather?* For real?"

The old man's eyes shimmered. He nodded. "Yep."

"Good God." A thousand questions swirled in Jace's mind. "But what—how?"

Artie shrugged. "I was married to Maudie. Anna understood. She didn't want to hurt her. Neither did I. Anna stayed because she and her father didn't agree about the baby. She needed a friend. And that was me. I couldn't marry her, but I could be there for Joyce, be her stand-in father. So that's what I was."

Jace tried to bend his mind around that. He remembered Joyce's mother. She'd been a teacher in the Elmer school. A widow, he'd always thought. Now he looked at Artie, feeling dazed.

Artie shook his head. "It coulda been different," he said. "I shoulda believed in her love. That's all I'm sayin'." He leaned forward again and fixed Jace with a steady stare. "You don't need my advice. When you find a love like that, you do exactly what you're doin', boy. You believe."

After the night at The Barrel, Celie didn't go home.

The house was full. Besides Polly and the kids, her other sister, Mary Beth, and her husband and their triplet daughters were coming up for the wedding.

"There's not going to be a wedding," Celie had insisted.

But Polly said, "When you mobilize triplets, you don't change your plans. Wedding or not, they're coming."

And, even later, a plane from Mexico would be bringing Sloan.

They could all visit. The triplets could play with Jack. Mary Beth and Polly would be glad to get together. They didn't see each other all that often. Tomorrow they could all go out and visit Joyce and Walt. A good time would be had by all.

They'd never miss the wedding that wasn't going to happen.

At least that's what Celie told herself late that night when everyone else had gone home and she checked herself into a motel room in Livingston.

It was a cold room with thin walls and even thinner carpet. Depressing. Grim. Looking exactly the way she felt, which was awful.

Why did she feel so bad? She was doing the right thing.

But Jace was going to be hurt.

He was going to show up for the wedding. He was going to stand up there in front of all those people and wait for her. It was going to be worse for him than it had been for her with Matt. She hadn't marched up the aisle. She'd taken his call privately. She hadn't had to make the announcement, face the crowd, see the pity, hear the snickers.

Not then.

Later, of course, she had. And she couldn't deny that it had hurt.

She didn't want Jace to be hurt. She loved him. That was the whole point of not marrying him.

Wasn't it?

Celie flung herself down on the bed. Oh, God. She didn't know anymore.

Was it Jace she was protecting? Or was it herself?

For years she would have loved to have made a fool of Jace. And he knew it. If he was everything she'd once thought he was, he would never make himself this vulnerable. He would never give her the chance. He'd be laughing at her—not giving her the chance to let the world laugh at him.

So why was he doing it?

Because he loved her. Really.

Celie rolled over and stared at the ceiling, letting the words enter her mind—and finally, enter her heart. She'd heard them; he'd said them.

But she hadn't really believed them before. Hadn't really understood them. Hadn't known how vulnerable they made him, hadn't realized the depth of his faith.

He loved her.

That meant he trusted her—not just for a week on a ship or the month of a fling—but forever. It meant Jace saw something in her, believed in something in her beyond even what she was capable of seeing.

He was right. It had nothing to do with Tamara. It was only about the two of them. About their faith in each other. Their trust in each other.

Celie knew that Jace believed.

The question was: did she?

''We look mighty handsome in these here tuxes,'' Artie said, studying Jace's white face and his own ruddy one in the mirror as they waited, resplendent in their formal finery in the room just behind the church.

They were all dressed up with just minutes to go—and Jace was feeling sicker by the second. He shouldn't have pushed her. He should have waited. Let her give him the ring back, courted her some more. Been persuasive. But he hadn't. He'd been his usual stubborn self—he'd pushed too hard, trusted too much and dared her when he never should have dared.

And now it was too late. He was committed. He had to go out there now and make an ass of himself. And Celie wasn't going to show up.

He'd seen Polly minutes before and she'd said she hadn't seen Celie since last night.

''What the hell do you mean you haven't seen her since last night? She lives with you!''

''She didn't come home after we went to The Barrel. Too many people,'' Polly apologized. ''Said she wanted some space. A motel room, I think. And no, not with another man,'' she said, grinning at his look of horror. ''It's just nerves, Jace.''

But it wasn't. It was more than nerves. Jace knew that now. Oh, God, oh, God, oh, God.

The organ music started. Jace, who had been counting hours up until last night, now wished he had a few hundred more.

''That's our cue.'' Artie poked him in the ribs.

Jace thought he might throw up. ''Artie, I—''

''Celie's a good gal,'' Artie said firmly. ''The best. Let's go. Sooner we go, sooner we can get you hitched. Sooner we get you hitched, sooner I can loosen my collar. I know I said I liked this tux, but goldarn it, boy, this necktie's durned near killin' me.''

With Artie at his side, Jace went to stand at the front of the church. It was full to bursting. Everyone who knew him, everyone who knew Celie was there. Alice and Cloris were right up front next to his sister's family. On the other side were Walt and Joyce; Walt's daughter, An, and her two children; Mary Beth and her husband, Jack, and the triplets. Taggart and Felicity Jones and their kids were there, as were the Tanners and McCalls, both the Nichols brothers and their families, plus Gus and Mary Holt. With them was Walt's younger daughter, Cait, holding her brand-new son, Andrew.

Jace didn't see Cait's husband, Charlie, until a flash went off. And he realized that he'd forgotten to contact a photographer. Or maybe he hadn't forgotten. Maybe it had been Freudian—not wanting the fiasco immortalized on film.

But whether he wanted it or not, Charlie was busy taking lots of photos of everyone who'd come to witness his marriage to Celie. Or not.

Oh, God. He didn't believe it. There, halfway back, was Tamara on Gavin's arm. She beamed at him and waggled her fingers. Jace shut his eyes. When he opened them again he spotted Celie's ship roommate, Allison, and that oily Armand and—good grief—Gloria Campanella!

And then the organ stopped. There was an intake of breath, a hush fell over everything—and then the minister appeared. The organist began "Here Comes the Bride," and Jace wanted to go through the floor.

Daisy was the first to come up the aisle, She wore a deep blue, floor-length gown, and she moved with careful, measured steps, at the speed of a snail. She was trying not to smile—or to frown—Jace wasn't sure which. She was managing to look worried all the same. After her came Lizzie, equally slowly, equally worried.

Jace felt ill.

Why the hell didn't they stop the wedding? If she wasn't there, why were they making him go through with this? They could say something, couldn't they?

Or was it up to him?

Sara was next. Her dress was like the others, but fuller to accommodate the burgeoning child. She looked beautiful, so like Celie that it hurt almost to look at her. She came down the aisle like a ship under full sail. Only when she got to the front did she look at Jace. She smiled at him, looking nervous. Looking worried.

And then came Polly, the matron of honor. Her riot of reddish-brown hair had been severely tamed and knotted elegantly on top of her head. She moved slowly, too, staring straight ahead, chin high.

Jace looked around her, trying to see behind her, daring to hope. But he didn't see Sloan. And he didn't see Celie.

Polly reached the front of the church. Her eyes met his, and he thought he saw sadness in them. But her chin stayed up, as if she were willing his to.

The organist played gamely on. And on. The congregation looked at Jace and everyone assembled at the front of the church, and then they looked toward the back. They began to murmur, to wonder...

And then...omigod...there she was!

Her hair was flying all over the place, her cheeks were bright red, and she was wearing jeans and a sweatshirt. But she was hanging on to a grinning Sloan's tux-clad arm and she was walking—not slowly at all—down the aisle to meet him!

The murmurs grew louder. The minister coughed. Artie cleared his throat. Polly and her daughters were caught between laughing and gaping. Charlie Seeks Elk was shooting a ton of pictures.

"I had a flat tire," Celie said for Jace's ears only, "after I got over my crisis of faith. But I'm here now and I'm ready if you are."

"I'm ready," Jace said, and took her hand in his.

The minister nodded. He smiled and gave a little shake of his head. "Dearly beloved, we are gathered here together..."

It was, in all, a wedding to remember.

They'd forgotten to plan a honeymoon.

"A guy can only think of so much," Jace explained as they stood in the kitchen of Polly's house late in the evening of their wedding day. The reception was over. The crowds had dispersed. Sloan and Polly and their bunch had gone one way, Mary Beth and her family had gone another. It was just the two of them. "Planning a wedding takes a lot out of a fellow."

"I did most of the work," Celie reminded him.

"Well, yeah," Jace agreed. "But only before you got cold feet."

"They're warm now," Celie assured him, waggling her toes.

Jace just grinned. "Prove it."

"I will," Celie promised. "As soon as we get to the cabin."

When the honeymoon lapse had been discovered, Taggart Jones had offered his cabin. "It's quiet. Isolated. Private."

"A perfect place for a honeymoon," Shane Nichols had said cheerfully with a wink at his wife, Poppy.

Celie hadn't understood that. "I thought he and Poppy went to Reno for theirs."

Jace didn't know. He didn't care. "Come on, then, let's go."

"I have to get packed and get changed."

"You look fine." She was wearing the jeans and sweatshirt she'd got married in. He, thank God, had changed out of his tux long ago.

"I'll be just a minute," Celie promised. She hurried upstairs.

Jace cooled his heels in the kitchen. In his mind he replayed the wedding. He saw Celie again in his mind's eye as he had seen her coming down the aisle. It was a vision he'd never forget. And it meant more to him than he could ever say.

She'd come to him as she was—because she loved him. The dress hadn't mattered. Perfection hadn't mattered. It was their love that had mattered.

Artie, the old son of a gun, had been right again—you just had to believe.

The sound of footsteps on the stairs caused him to turn around. His jaw dropped. He stared.

Celie was coming down the stairs in her wedding dress.

All of it. Yards and yards and yards of it. She looked ravishing, astonishing, utterly beautiful. And wholly inappropriate.

Jace, grinning, said, "What the hell are you doin'? We're goin' up to the back of the beyond!"

But Celie shrugged happily. "Well, I couldn't not wear it, could I? Besides, I couldn't let you off the hook completely."

"Huh?"

"Every man needs a challenge," Celie told him, sliding her arms around him, kissing him and fanning the flames of desire.

"Challenge?" Jace said warily.

Celie grinned. "Only forty or fifty buttons or so."

*   *   *   *   *

Don't miss the next special installment
in Anne McAllister's fabulous
CODE OF THE WEST *series.*

THE COWBOY'S CHRISTMAS MIRACLE

Available in December 2002,
only from Silhouette Special Edition.

And don't miss
THE GREAT MONTANA COWBOY AUCTION
available now from Silhouette books.

presents

A brand-new miniseries about the Connellys of Chicago,
a wealthy, powerful American family tied by blood to the
royal family of the island kingdom of Altaria.
They're wealthy, powerful and rocked by
scandal, betrayal…and passion!

Look for a whole year of glamorous and
utterly romantic tales in 2002:

Where love comes alive™

If you enjoyed what you just read,
then we've got an offer you can't resist!

Take 2 bestselling love stories FREE!

Plus get a FREE surprise gift!

Clip this page and mail it to Silhouette Reader Service™

IN U.S.A.
3010 Walden Ave.
P.O. Box 1867
Buffalo, N.Y. 14240-1867

IN CANADA
P.O. Box 609
Fort Erie, Ontario
L2A 5X3

YES! Please send me 2 free Silhouette Desire® novels and my free surprise gift. After receiving them, if I don't wish to receive anymore, I can return the shipping statement marked cancel. If I don't cancel, I will receive 6 brand-new novels every month, before they're available in stores! In the U.S.A., bill me at the bargain price of $3.34 plus 25¢ shipping and handling per book and applicable sales tax, if any*. In Canada, bill me at the bargain price of $3.74 plus 25¢ shipping and handling per book and applicable taxes**. That's the complete price and a savings of at least 10% off the cover prices—what a great deal! I understand that accepting the 2 free books and gift places me under no obligation ever to buy any books. I can always return a shipment and cancel at any time. Even if I never buy another book from Silhouette, the 2 free books and gift are mine to keep forever.

225 SEN DFNS
326 SEN DFNT

Name	(PLEASE PRINT)	
Address	Apt.#	
City	State/Prov.	Zip/Postal Code

* Terms and prices subject to change without notice. Sales tax applicable in N.Y.
** Canadian residents will be charged applicable provincial taxes and GST.
All orders subject to approval. Offer limited to one per household and not valid to current Silhouette Desire® subscribers.
® are registered trademarks of Harlequin Enterprises Limited.

DES01 ©1998 Harlequin Enterprises Limited

magazine

♥ quizzes

Is he the one? What kind of lover are you? Visit the **Quizzes** area to find out!

♥ recipes for romance

Get scrumptious meal ideas with our **Recipes for Romance.**

♥ romantic movies

Peek at the **Romantic Movies** area to find Top 10 Flicks about First Love, ten Supersexy Movies, and more.

♥ royal romance

Get the latest scoop on your favorite royals in **Royal Romance.**

♥ games

Check out the **Games** pages to find a ton of interactive romantic fun!

♥ romantic travel

In need of a romantic rendezvous? Visit the **Romantic Travel** section for articles and guides.

♥ lovescopes

Are you two compatible? Click your way to the **Lovescopes** area to find out now!

Silhouette® —

where love comes alive—online...

SINTMAG

Continues the captivating series from
bestselling author

BARBARA McCAULEY

SECRETS!

Hidden legacies, hidden loves—revel in the
unfolding of the Blackhawk siblings' deepest, most
desirable SECRETS!

Don't miss the next irresistible books in the series...

TAMING BLACKHAWK
On Sale May 2002
(SD #1437)

IN BLACKHAWK'S BED
On Sale July 2002
(SD #1447)

And look for another title on sale in 2003!

Available at your favorite retail outlet.

Where love comes alive™

**Where royalty and romance
go hand in hand...**

The series continues in Silhouette Romance
with these unforgettable novels:

HER ROYAL HUSBAND
by Cara Colter
on sale July 2002 (SR #1600)

THE PRINCESS HAS AMNESIA!
by Patricia Thayer
on sale August 2002 (SR #1606)

SEARCHING FOR HER PRINCE
by Karen Rose Smith
on sale September 2002 (SR #1612)

And look for more Crown and Glory stories in
SILHOUETTE DESIRE starting in October 2002!

Available at your favorite retail outlet.

Visit Silhouette at www.eHarlequin.com   SRCAG

COMING NEXT MONTH

SDCNM0602